The Ecstasy of Dr Miriam Garner

ELAINE FEINSTEIN

The Ecstasy of
Dr Miriam Garner

HUTCHINSON OF LONDON

Hutchinson & Co (Publishers) Ltd
3 Fitzroy Square, London W1

London Melbourne Sydney Auckland
Wellington Johannesburg and agencies
throughout the world

First published 1976
© Elaine Feinstein 1976

Set in Intertype Baskerville

Printed in Great Britain by
The Anchor Press Ltd and bound by
Wm Brendon & Son Ltd
both of Tiptree, Essex

ISBN 0 09 126670 X

For Arnold

I

—Baker. Where are you now, Baker? Have you dropped yet?

—We got a bit a traffic.

The cab stood pinned between cars wedged wheel to wheel the length of Euston Road. Dr Miriam Garner put two ginger boots on the folding seat ahead of her, took a powder compact of the Marlene Dietrich era from her bag, and searched her impassive Inca face for signs of fatigue. It was a pity, she reflected, that London's summer rainlight should bring out the yellow in her tan. Otherwise, she looked much as she had leaving New York. She snapped the small pewter case shut, with a precise, satisfied click; looked sideways at her companion, Bernard Hill, and was surprised to see him perched on the edge of his seat and sweating in visible alarm.

—I'm afraid you'll miss your train, said Bernard, as if embarrassed by his own anxiety.

Miriam observed him with a cool detachment that almost amounted to rudeness. How could she ever have been in love with this paunching stranger? The thin yellow silk of his hair was beginning to fail, and his bald patch was pink and wet. He looked far older than thirty-five. Had she really fought to hold him through the whole of one grubby March and snowy April years ago? The episode seemed as unlikely now as Harriet's plump and smiling victory.

—Poor Bernard, she said.

A little mischievously she reasoned out the source of

7

his unease. Maybe he had concealed his journey to Heathrow from Harriet; perhaps he was already late for some meeting with his family?

—Try one of these, she suggested, offering him a pill bottle. Bernard looked at her outstretched hand with disgust.

—Tranquillizers, he said : are a sign of moral weakness.

—I wouldn't exactly call this a tranquillizer, she murmured : But I do remember. It was all health food and meditation when I left. Does Harriet still go to Yoga classes?

—Unfortunately, Harriet has slipped a disc, said Bernard formally : I must say *you* look well enough. In your letter you spoke of sick leave.

—Well, I have been in hospital, said Miriam.

—Nothing too serious evidently.

The cab crawled a few yards forward. Everwhere the air was heavy and wet; the sky lay over the buzzing cars like greasy wool.

—Why are you smiling? asked Bernard.

—I'm not.

After five years they seemed to have little to say to one another, she thought. Miriam didn't mind. They had travelled in peaceful silence most of the way from the airport. But now the traffic trap had Bernard casting about for conversation.

—Have you kept on your loft in the Bowery? he asked.

Miriam said : I let it out for six months. Just in case.

Then she stopped as if deciding against telling a longer story.

—Stavros left, she said, with apparent inconsequence : He went to L.A. Did you hear?

—No.

—We split.

—I'm sorry.

—It was time, she said.

8

—Well Stavros, said Bernard : I know.

Miriam laughed, rather unkindly. Because Bernard absolutely did not know. He might *imagine* he knew Stavros because they had once shared College rooms; certainly he admired Stavros and probably even thought Stavros liked him, or respected him; which was amusing.

Bernard watched her laughter with some alarm.

—I'm sorry, she said, biting her lip : I don't mean to.

—You get through a lot of men, said Bernard.

Miriam thought about that.

—Yes, she admitted : I'm not a good woman, am I? It's because I don't like being eaten alive. Isn't that what goodness means in a woman? Even Stavros put two years of my life into his mouth without tasting them. Anyway I'm finished with all that.

Bernard grunted sceptically.

—Yes, I am. I know now. I'm a natural spinster.

—Baker? said the radio voice querulously.

The sky had darkened. Suddenly a forest of thick white rain flooded down over the trapped cars. The noise and blindness together was bewildering for a few moments, until gradually headlights came on, pair by pair, looking like round, yellow eyes half-drowned in the spurting water.

Miriam sat up and rubbed the glass to see more clearly : What a fabulous storm, she said.

—I'm still stifling, muttered Bernard.

A pause lay awkwardly between them again, which Bernard evidently felt it was his duty to alleviate.

—I read your monograph on translation, he said finally.

—Did you?

—Yes. On the Toledo Manuscripts? He seemed to be trying desperately to nudge her into passing comment : Fascinating, I thought.

—Yes, she said.

9

Somehow she could not make any effort to help the conversation forward. If anything she felt slightly irritated; as if his interest in her work were a form of trespass.

—I have no Arabic myself, he said apologetically.

—Why should you?

Bernard tried again.

—Did I tell you I saw your father on the telly a few weeks ago? Quite by chance.

Miriam's head swung round at once. He had a sense that for the first time he had captured her full attention, and he became almost garrulous in relief.

—Yes. Rather surprising. It was just a chat show. But there he was. Prof Octavius Garner in all his splendour. She said: How was he? On the box I mean.

—Much himself. Bossy. Sarcastic. Not quite so rude, I suppose. Perhaps they edited the tape.

—Yes. When was all this?

—Last term, I think.

—I thought it couldn't be very recent.

She lay back again and closed her eyes. The traffic was beginning to move. In a few moments, she thought, they would reach the station.

—Miriam, she could hear an old voice on the transatlantic phone: I'm confused, Mirrie. Your poor Dad's losing control.

She had never heard him talk like that. It was impossible to imagine. However often he had changed direction however late a beginner in a new field, he had never thought of being wrong. Things always went the way he expected. He'd always bounced with the certainty of miracles in his favour.

—I'm an old man now. I can't fight any more.

Leaning back, with her eyes shut, Miriam wondered

with a sliver of fear in her chest, what her father could possibly be fighting.

Bernard's voice roused her, tinged with impatience as if he had been speaking a long time : You must have *some* idea where you are going.

—Of course, she stared at him : Didn't I tell you? Cambridge. I shall find a nice quiet cell there.

—And then?

—I shall read books, and think.

—Won't that be rather boring?

—People are bored by different things, Bernard. Don't you know that? What do *you* do at the weekends? Decorate the house? Take the kids out? Now that *would* have me screaming.

—Reading books isn't enough, he said doggedly : Whatever you say.

—Then I shall have a rest.

And now they were driving into King's Cross. Miriam said nothing more. She turned her head and kissed Bernard on his ear, lightly, as a farewell.

—It isn't every day, she said, following her own thoughts. Bernard looked at her queerly.

—Well, is it? she asked, puzzled.

The rain had stopped, the sky broken. For a moment she recalled her last time in England. It was in February and she remembered her sense of a numinous world present in light that rose as the earth turned. There was snow on the wet brown streets then; yes, she remembered looking out from the window of her father's house at the frozen glass of the conservatory; there were green and orange leaves on the creepers. Everywhere else was brown. Dry copper bunches on the lilac, rusty brown leaves. She drew in her breath sharply as a familiar bodiless unease took hold of her. A nun, that's what Stavros had shouted. Nonsense, because the Church had no attraction for her. Even its architecture, even those glowing windows of Chartres, were unconnected with her sense of numinous presence. Only once, in a mosque at Acco, when a man in white had broken off a scented branch, and blessed her, had she experienced the faintest touch of religious belief. She smiled.

—I want you to know, said Bernard, looking straight ahead and totally unaware of her thoughts : Harriet and I are extremely happy.

As the glass and steel doors of the newly built station parted at her approach, Miriam walked firmly between them, carrying a single white suitcase, and fully aware of the striking figure she made. It was partly her height, partly her haughty carriage; but mostly the superb cut of her clothes. Her skirt was chastely dark and low in the calf; but snugly fitted to the line of her buttocks. Eyes followed her with a kind of stunned envy.

She went to discover when the next train for Cambridge would leave.

—Seven minutes, platform 9, said the clerk behind the counter : It's the other bit of the station, Miss. The dirty bit. Walk down to where it says Toilets, if you'll excuse me, and turn sharp left.

—I remember, said Miriam : I wonder if I've got time to buy a paper?

—If you scuttle, said the clerk.

Miriam thanked him. But she didn't scuttle. Instead she walked slowly in the direction he had pointed out, leaving the new white airport-style shops behind her, and was soon in the familiar stink and dinge of an older London twenty-five years gone; the air tasting of diesel. The train was in, and she mounted it at once. It was as squalid as the platform. She opened carriage after carriage all smelling like telephone boxes. The cushions puffed out dust as she touched them. There was no buffet

car. At length she opened a door at random, found herself
a corner seat and wriggled into a position she could
sleep. She was feeling faintly ill-tempered. The meeting
with Bernard had hardly been a success. Not that she'd
wanted to get close to him; but there he was, with a piece
of her past self still connected to him. And totally remote
from her.

Even as she settled she was joined by two men, one
with a high bald head and flushed cheeks; and the other
dressed in white cricketing clothes, and carrying a
mackintosh. Covertly she watched and placed them,
even before they began to talk.

—The women's Colleges don't want it either.

—It isn't a question of justice.

—Naturally not. People are totally confused.

—No woman worth her salt.

—Exactly.

Sleep arrived slowly. Her mind wandered; she was
walking up Petty Cury as she had last seen it, dark and
wet, with yellow pavements, and rain and clay running
under the fence where a huge crane hung over what
remained of Barclays Bank. Then it was mid-May; and
there were cherry petals lying like snow in the gutter,
gradually turning brown. She dropped with their darkening through several levels of consciousness but she could
not enter the blackness of sleep.

Turning her head to one side, she carefully adjusted
the brightly coloured silk at her neck to hide the green
thumb-print of a bruise Stavros had given her months
before. And she smiled with a certain satisfaction at her
own restraint in the taxi. Bernard abhorred violence.
There *had* been one moment, when she had imagined
his kind brown eyes opening in incredulity as she told
him a few bare facts about her life with Stavros. With
some relish, she had thought of his expression turning

13

to bewilderment. He deserved to feel bewildered, she thought; but probably he would have quickly translated that emotion into pity for her which she did not want. She could never explain the good times, she thought, with a certain sexual nostalgia; even if Stavros had bullied her mercilessly and once banged her head so hard with a marble figurine she had to be X-rayed, to look for brain damage. *Brain damage.* Even now she couldn't remember that week. She had been conscious and aware; but not exactly awake. Concussed, possibly. She lay more or less motionless and sleepless, without curiosity, impetus or any motive for action. Her indifference amounted almost to insubstantiality. She knew they were taking her E.E.G. But she was too shut in cold hopelessness to argue, or refer them to the notes from her Los Angeles doctor. She just let them go through all the tests again. She hadn't even the sense of loss that might have been expected. Most patients looked back to their time before hospital as some kind of enchanted, unblemished state; but she didn't feel there was any loss of primal, happy innocence. She didn't even look *forward* to redemption from the state she had fallen into. Some of the treatment was unpleasant; they gave her a drug which made her limbs ache, and she was very glad when they stopped that. But there was one perfect day, so peaceful, she could only remember it with envy, when she seemed to have fallen into a radiance she had never felt in the dingy world outside. Of course, it was only one day. Most days, it was a question of gradually recovering the power over her limbs; marvelling at the return of function to an elbow joint or a leg muscle. And still she hadn't particularly longed for normality.

She knew Stavros came to see her most days; though they wouldn't let him in, and she neither cared that he was coming nor felt any anger towards him.

At length, they stopped sedating her at night; and

reality, if that was the word for a six-by-four white cell, returned as sharply, as if it had never left her. With amusement she saw the doctors didn't know why her senses had returned; any more than they understood what had happened in the first place.

Concussion; no brain damage; query epilepsy. Discharge. That would do for the records.

What she remembered clearly was Stavros when she came out. He was so kind; it almost made her miss him, just to think of it. He cooked her steaks, and brought her coffee in bed. For one whole week that was, until he caught her reading. And then he took the book away and said : My god, you're skiving off back into the past again. What's the matter with you? Why can't you just *be* here and now? With me?

And she said : Look, this *is* me just being. This is what I'm like. I read books.

At which he was so enraged he dropped the book right on her. Not once. Twice. And that was the bruise. Well, he was a very difficult man. You couldn't live with a man like that. Not that there was a man she could live with probably; most were either dull or desperate. And she almost enjoyed being lonely. All the space of it. She wasn't like one of those terrifying deserted wives, dammit; weeping into their coffee, and complaining it was better to have someone die than be rejected.

Miriam looked out of the window at the countryside where the trees were still black even in May. There were a few clouds. Yellow gorse everywhere. Puddles of rain in the hollows. Wherever she looked, there were deserts of rubble; huge reels for electric cables lay about empty and rotten as old barrels. And the stations with their lavatory-tiled waiting rooms and brown benches could only belong to this penurious Eastern region.

15

A kind of animosity built up in her at the contrast with the prosperous areas of America. She resented returning across this desolate county where the only colours were the yellow of cranes, with broken hooks hanging from them; and red cement-mixers. Even the trucks in the sidings looked broken down to her. And the allotments had a dismal, post-war pathos; with the cellophane torn over the tomato-beds.

CAMBRIDGE, the signs said in capitals. CAMBRIDGE. And she felt an odd pang at the expectation the word set up, half-expecting to see her father at the ticket box waiting for her. But there was no-one she knew. It was still raining. She was lucky to get a taxi.

Her father's house had been built in the middle of the nineteenth century for a prosperous draper in what must have been fields at the southern extremity of the town. Meaner houses had caught up with its magnificence. It stood now behind a thicket hedge, which *had* been trim, Miriam recalled, but with branches now jutting out so far it was almost impossible to walk along the pavement without being slapped in the face by them. Uneasily, Miriam took in other signs that the house had been allowed to fall into decay. There were trees growing into the drooping Virginia creeper which covered one side of the house; untrimmed clematis that had once so elegantly framed the ironwork arch above the door dangled broken into the flower beds. The flowers of unused Jerusalem artichokes (looking like hollyhocks) grew close to the wall of the house; in places the signs of damp were visible in the discoloured bricks. The peeling green door had not been painted for a decade and grass, moss and even roots had distorted the paving stones which led in a path to the front door.

But the house was clearly occupied. Light streamed out, not only from the window over the door, but also through a grating between the steps, where the largely unused cellars could be dimly guessed at. As she stood, pulling at the old bell, hearing its familiar sound, she became conscious of an almost overpowering odour of crushed lavender, and she saw that the branch of a maple tree, for some reason sawn off, was now lying across a lavender bush.

It was not her father but a girl who opened the door.

—Dr Miriam Garner, is it?

—Yes.

Miriam eyed the girl doubtfully. Her father had written of a housekeeper, but nothing in his letter suggested the strange quality of the woman she now faced. Her face had the unmarked, unlined quality of a girl of twelve or thirteen; yet her voice was as slow and deep as a woman of thirty. The eyes were almost of the colour of bluebells; and her features small and podgy. Her limbs and especially her wrists and legs were frail to the point of emaciation; almost as if she was suffering from some kind of wasting disease.

Miriam entered past her into the large hall, which had always been cold even in summer, but now smelt not of polish, as she remembered it, but a kind of blue mouldering.

—I've got some food on a tray for you, said the girl.

—Where is my father?

—In bed. Asleep. He said not to wake him. He *did* wait up for you, said the girl: My name's Cressida.

—I'm not hungry.

Miriam walked past her angrily into the kitchen; a large room, it had once been immaculate and now was faintly musty. A tray with sandwiches stood on the table, with a thermos flask.

—It's a big house to look after, said Miriam: You really don't look as if you could possibly cope with the work.

—Well, I have to be *with* him, don't I? said the girl.

17

When she spoke her shoulders curved inward with a cringing movement. Nevertheless there was something insolent in her reply. Miriam saw that her greasy brown hair was secured by a single schoolgirl kirby grip.

—Are you a nurse? asked Miriam acidly.

The flapping crooked hands gave a jerk of denial, but the face showed no sign of irritation.

—Perhaps I'll have a coffee, said Miriam : Not from a thermos, however, thank you. I'll make my own, if you'll show me the beans.

The girl's left shoulder went up in a shrug, and she began to look sullen.

—Please yourself. There aren't any beans though.

—Ground coffee then.

—There's Nescafé.

Miriam stared.

—My father always insisted on real coffee.

—It's bad for him.

Miriam opened the thermos and poured herself a drink.

—Is my bed made up?

—Yes.

—I'll go upstairs then. Please stop hovering round me. I know the way.

The girl picked up with surprising ease the heavy leather suitcase Miriam had brought in, panting; and Miriam registered that the matchstick arms plainly had more strength than she realized.

—You're in the guest room, said Cressida.

—What? Why not my old room? asked Miriam.

—All my things in there, aren't they? said the girl.

—You sleep in my room?

—Well, it's closer. In case he calls. In the night.

—But you knew I was coming! It was unimaginative if not even rude, said Miriam brusquely.

She followed the girl past her old bedroom with

particular distaste, repelled at the thought of the creature sleeping in her bed.

—The lodger's room got a basin, said the girl: We had it put in.

—Then you should find it very comfortable, said Miriam: You'll please pack your clothes tomorrow and prepare to change the sheets, and we'll exchange rooms early tomorrow morning.

The girl said nothing. She put down the cases and waited.

—Do go away, said Miriam: Can't you see I just want to be left alone?

For a moment, she was tempted to go and have a look at her father, and see if he really was asleep as the girl had said. But a certain guilt about her late arrival prevented her. Perhaps it had been inconsiderate. It was hard to remember her father was an old man.

—The doctor's coming in the morning, volunteered the girl, who had not moved.

—The doctor?

—That's right. Your father don't always see him, but he's due for a visit then.

—Then I hope you'll get to work, before he comes. Dusting about, said Miriam sharply: The place is a filthy shambles. Aren't you ashamed?

—I don't bother much about the doctor, said the girl. Miriam stared at her again, troubled. She had put an edge on her voice that reached through most skins. For a second she wondered if the girl was mentally defective.

—I read your books, said Cressida: You writing another one while you're here?

—Perhaps, said Miriam, unable to disguise her surprise.

—You'll have to help you know. I can't do anything with his papers.

—For God's sake, said Miriam: What on earth? How dare you meddle with his papers?

19

—Well, *he* can't do it. Can't even do the maths now. The proofs were bad enough.

Miriam went to the door and opened it firmly: To-morrow. We'll talk about it tomorrow. You certainly must *not* meddle with his papers.

The physical disgust she felt for this curiously disabled girl, and her jerky almost spidery movements was made the more uncomfortable by some recognition she could not at first articulate. It was familiar, as a parody is familiar, but uneasily just out of the reach of memory.

As she was putting on a nightgown she almost placed it; but it fluked out of reach. *Maths?* She found herself thinking instead. What was he up to? Had she seen his new book advertised? Perhaps. But most of his pioneer work had already been taken up on the West Coast. It was hard to believe he had found anything new. She sat on the bed for a moment, depressed with the certainty of wasted effort. Then she resolutely opened the sheets, and lay down.

As she was dropping off to sleep a sudden sharp vision of herself as an adolescent; gawky, with stooped and book-ish shoulders, helplessly trying on a lamé dress under the eye of a contemptuous shop assistant came into her mind. She pushed it back irritably. But it returned, more spidery, with an even younger face. Yes, she was at her own twelfth birthday party, crying in a corner; grimly sure of her own ugliness, ill-developed breasts, and thick waist. The misery pierced her so sharply it woke her in the darkness. And then with sudden clarity she placed the memory that had plagued her earlier. The loathsome Cressida reminded her of nothing so much as her own submerged and forgotten self.

Altogether the night passed restlessly. Occasionally Miriam woke with a jolt that set her heart banging. Towards morning, she sat up resignedly, put on the bedside lamp, and stared round her. The night before she had only noticed the dinginess of the room; now the grotesque heterogeneity of the contents struck her with disquiet. On an old, disconnected gas-cooker sheets of typed papers were bundled in polythene bags which had been knotted like laundry sacks. Even the drawers of her bedside chest lay open; and discarded clothes and blankets hung out of every one of them. As she moved the lamp at her side, Miriam almost knocked over a sepia photograph, standing without its glass. In it, a tender-faced woman with deep-lidded, mournful eyes, held up an unfamiliar blob of a child towards her. For a moment Miriam stared wonderingly into the woman's face, which had the gentle beauty of Holbein's Lais of Corinth. A sorrowful lady in a brown garden, she stirred Miriam's memory uneasily with odours of ginger, cinnamon and rose-water. Momentarily, Miriam imagined her move, with one arm in long-sleeved emerald silk extended, beckoning. But then she was sepia again, like the paper grass she sat on, back inside the silver frame of her photograph. Miriam's attention was caught by a school exercise book in an immature handwriting she took to be her own. This she picked up, with a half-smile; and began to read, at first with little more than casual curiosity. Then all at once she was seized with a fever of excitement and her fingers began to tremble, because the many closely written pages had been written by someone else.

The town was biscuit coloured, she read, *seen from the road beside the Tagus. The long horizon of eroded mountains lay behind, bare and uninhabited; even though aromatic plants grew on the upper slopes. At the roadside, exhausted by hunger and thirst, a family lay sheltering as best they could from the sun and waiting for the heat to drop from its afternoon height.*

2

The strongest-looking man among them had the arms and chest of an artisan; he lay on his back with an elbow across his eyes, sleeping. Beside him a woman kept awake, her sharp features and leather skin ageless, as she ran her reddened eyes over their meagre possessions. The few donkeys tethered nearby carried only cooking pots and a few dried pieces of meat. The bundles beside her looked like rags. Yet she kept guard over them as if she had bartered a house for each donkey, and a vineyard for every piece of cloth. Occasionally, she looked expressionlessly towards a man with hair like grey wire who looked so shrivelled that he could have been taken for dead, except that occasionally the limbs of his left side twitched in sleep. A few children had been cradled lovingly in shabby wickerwork; and one or two adolescents waking from time to time spoke to one another in Arabic; always with their eyes on the watchful woman, and in low careful tones.

They too fell silent as two horsemen approached from beyond the hill, wearing jewelled daggers. As if at a signal, the woman shook the arm of the sleeping man at her side. His eyes opened, though he remained still. The two men reigned in their animals briefly and looked at the family without much interest. But then the younger man pointed away from the donkeys, beyond the figure of the old man, to where among the rags and *sambanitos,* lay one coloured silk dress about the body of a young girl more firmly fleshed than the others and lying apart

22

from them. The two men exchanged glances as they looked down on her.

At once the girl's eyes opened and she sat up with an abrupt movement, staring wildly about her at the desolate scene, and looking at the other sleeping creatures near her with astonished horror.

—Where are you from? asked the younger horseman courteously.

She shook her head in bewilderment.

—Perhaps she doesn't speak Castilian, Luis. Try Arabic. It is the language of the *aljamas,* suggested his friend. The girl continued to stare at them with sullen eyes : No need, she said.

—These are all Toledano. Your accent is not like theirs. Where are you from? repeated Luis.

—I can't tell you, she replied slowly : What I do not know.

—Then say where are you making for? asked Luis impatiently : All of you.

—Wake one of those creatures and ask she said : I know less than you where they hope to be going.

—Why, have you dropped from the sky? Or what would you have us believe? Luis' companion spoke roughly, as if the poverty and roughness of the wretches asleep on the ground alarmed him particularly.

In an undertone he said to his companion : Be careful; they are not all feeble, these runaways.

—But surely she is obviously from a good family?

Luis went over to the nearest man and shook him awake. He had a long, fine-featured face and red hair. Though he held his head low, there were lines of amusement at his eyes which suggested he had no trouble in placing Luis, and perhaps even knew his name. Asked about the girl, however, he protested total ignorance; indeed her presence seemed to alarm him. One or two of his brothers also waking up, stared across at her resentfully.

—Perhaps, said Luis, turning away from the shrewd

23

eyes of the red-haired man : She is running away to join a lover? Is it something of this kind, Señora? he asked hopefully.

—Where does this road lead? she asked without reply, gathering her hair into a sweep with a comb, and standing, he now saw, some three inches taller than was usual for a woman.

—We are going towards Toledo, said Luis.

—Then I will come with you.

—Tell me first, said Luis' companion urgently : Are you an old Christian? You are not dressed like a Moor. Perhaps you are a Hebrew?

At this question a cackling laugh rose from the watchful old woman on the road, and Luis turned with surprise towards her. It was the red-haired man, however, who spoke for her, in explanation : She was telling us a story about her father who had three pairs of pigeons, Señor, he said, and he spoke now in Castilian as fine as the ornately dressed young men : Before we left he showed her the first pair. They were ragged, but their wings were free and they flew. The second pair had their wings horribly mutilated. There was no question of flying anywhere; though they might hobble a little, and peck at what food they could find.

—And the third pair?

—The third pair were dead, Señor.

Luis Mesa's face darkened with wrath, and for a moment he looked as though he would have struck the young man.

—Leave him, said the girl sharply : The old woman may speak truly.

—What's this, said the young man : Sorcery?

—Isn't it foolish, she said indifferently : To kill those who may speak the truth?

—To read the stars is a matter of skill, and requires many instruments, said Luis gently.

24

To this she only replied obliquely : The moonlight is blue, here in the desert. Even the land is whitened by it, is that not so? But you understand nothing of how. All your instruments are play things.

—At best she is mad, said Luis' companion. Both men stared incredulously, and uneasily : These are not matters for teasing. She is strange, and her voice has authority. She will not pass unnoticed in Toledo.

—Nevertheless, let us take her with us, said Luis doggedly: If she will trust *me* enough to tell her name, I will trust her.

But before the young woman could speak the wretches who had been quietly gathering their baggage together, turned towards her; and a windless ripple of air carried the colours of her silk dress out so that for a moment it veiled even the luminous blue sky and the city that lay beyond.

—Ah, they cried together, gazing on her height and her beauty : Look!

—She is an Angel, shrieked one : She has come to deliver our people.

And for a moment it seemed as if all of them would cluster round her. But the young woman's voice rang out with savagery : No. No. Get away from me, all of you. There is no-one who will deliver you. Don't be deluded. Go on your way, though you meet only enemies. I cannot help you.

They murmured and shuffled, but her eyes flashed at them with such fury, that even the old woman and the sardonic red-haired youth had no choice but to turn their backs and be off.

—Now. Take me to Toledo, she said to Luis : I have been told it is a great city, with many towers, galleries and minarets.

—Assuredly, said Luis : And we live in peace. Last year we honoured Alphonso himself; Christians, Saracens and

Jews together, with lutes and citharas and drums, and we all sang praises to God in our own languages.

—And do you eat together?

—With tact, certainly. For my uncle's wedding, a Jewish butcher slaughtered a cow for his Jewish friends.

—And do you marry one another?

Luis frowned: That is always another matter.

His companion had fallen into a morose silence, as he watched his friend leading the horse upon which the strange lady rode with such ease. Presently they came to a crossroads, and he said abruptly: With your permission, Luis, I will take my farewell of you here.

Luis Mesa bowed, and watched him ride swiftly away.

—Why is he afraid Luis? she asked: Do you know?

—He is afraid of you, I think.

—There you are wrong, she said narrowing her eyes on the city before her.

Miriam must have fallen asleep some time after reading the last few sentences, for the book had slipped from her hand as daylight reached the bed, and she became conscious of Cressida standing by her side and holding a breakfast tray.

—You were staring at me. Before I woke up, said Miriam angrily, for some reason disliking the thought of those flower-like eyes on her sleeping face.

—I like to see people sleep, said Cressida: You can tell things. You looked frightened and unhappy, did you know that? You had two lines. There.

She put a finger towards Miriam's cheek.

—Well, said Miriam: I slept badly here. Please don't hang over me. From now on I'll make my own breakfast, thank you. Would you please begin to get my own room ready?

The girl lingered.

26

—I could tidy up more in here, she offered: I have to get up in the night, that's the thing. How will I hear his bell?

—Just leave that to me, said Miriam crisply, cutting into her eggs with a good appetite.

—Anyway your father wants to see you now, said Cressida, without moving.

—Shan't be long. I hope he is well this morning.

—Not so very. He is worried about his work.

Miriam paused on a mouthful of coffee, and remembered the story she had read in the night. Looking by the bed, she saw the exercise book lay there as it had fallen.

—Tell me, she said: What did you do before you took this job with my father?

—Studied, a bit.

—Where?

—Here.

—At the University?

In spite of herself, and five years of American training, Miriam could not keep the implicit snobbery out of her voice.

—I didn't finish, said Cressida: Because I was ill.

Her left shoulder contorted in what might have been a shrug.

—They said I was very bright at school. Well, I just like to help out now. Your father's been very good to me, you see. I think he feels responsible.

—How do you mean? asked Miriam sharply.

—For me, said Cressida, simply.

—Oh yes, well, for god's sake get along, said Miriam irritably: Please tell my father I'll just wash and get dressed, will you?

In about half an hour, spruce and elegant in beige linen, Miriam found herself hesitating irrationally outside her father's door. It seemed absurd to knock, as if a stranger lay inside; and yet a degree of strangeness made it impossible to call a greeting. In the event, there was no reply either to her knock or her voice; and so she opened the door gingerly.

At once an overpoweringly sweet odour filled her nostrils. She found it hard to place. Synthetic air-freshener perhaps? And yet there was a musty undertang of some human odour. Not sweat. Not urine. Something closer to the smell of unwashed clothes. Yet sweet. A vase of geraniums stood in a blue ceramic jar close to the doorway.

Her father was sitting up against his pillows with a shabby dressing-gown of mouse-grey flannel round his shoulders, but his glasses had fallen on to the bed, and he was evidently asleep. He had not yet shaved, and an extensive white stubble pushed through his pink flesh. Miriam stared at him almost without recognition. His mouth had fallen in, because he was not wearing his teeth. She found herself most reluctant to wake him.

As she made to leave, however, his eyes opened quickly; and she could see they were clear and black; though a little wild, like an angry horse.

—Is that you? he said.

—Miriam. Yes. I'm here.

—Come closer. I feel so terrible. I'm ill, Miriam. Help me.

—What do you want? asked Miriam, hypnotized into stillness.

—Make me comfortable. Move my pillow. Get me a cup of tea. Where are my pills?

An array of small bottles littered the bedside table.

—Give me the glass by the bed. Yes, that one. Change the water, will you? It smells funny. And I don't like the glass. Find one of the plain glasses. Downstairs.

—I can't do all that at once, cried Miriam in distress.

The old man fumbled for his glasses, in the half-light.
—Why don't you draw the curtains? she asked him.
—My eyes are weak.
—Open a window at least. There's no air in here. Those heavy curtains would make anyone feel ill. Do you realize it's a hot sunny day outside?
—The sun is bad for me.
—I'll get you a drink, she said.

She stared at him again. It was not that he had altogether changed in his *tone*; nevertheless the syntax had an alien child-like quality. And the heat in the room was unbearable. She was sweating as she came out of the sick man's room on to the square landing; and she threw open the window overlooking the garden. There were the familiar yellow maples, the old gnarled plum tree, and at the back a jungle of brambles that had once been elaborately pruned gooseberry and raspberry bushes. She breathed in deeply, with relief, even as she saw that no vegetables grew now in the open soil, which had run to grass; and the lawn itself was dry and yellow, with a few clumps of yellow stalks sticking up. Suddenly her attention halted. In the centre of the lawn, in a deck chair sitting with her eyes closed was Cressida.

—Miriam, where have you gone? I'm thirsty, remember?
—Coming, she replied automatically, drenched at the same time with a sharp flow of prickling anger at the injustice of having Cressida at her ease while she ran up and downstairs.

Down the stairs she went nevertheless, but on an impulse paused to look through the door to the conservatory. For a moment she took in the rows of tomato pots, with the neglected straw from seasons past still hanging dead on supporting wires, and smelt the harsh tobacco tang of her childhood; remembered the night-time watering of the plants, and the great hot red globes

29

of fruit when the sun beat through the glass. The sun was suffocatingly hot, even today; but several panes of glass were broken. The peach tree, which rose out of grey unwatered sand, was not however, completely dead she saw. A few shoots of this year's green had appeared on it. Reluctantly, she left the tree, and was turning across the hall towards the kitchen, when she heard the front door key in the lock. Miriam stopped and watched; could there be other occupants of the house? Lodgers perhaps?

The woman who came through, however, was a reassuring figure, inordinately large in the upper arm. She exposed a floral apron, in one great bustling movement, as she took off her outer coat.

—Good morning, said Miriam clearly, not wishing to startle the woman. But there was no sign that her presence was anything unusual.

—Morning, morning, said the woman moving straight past her into the kitchen, without pausing to enquire further. Miriam followed fascinated, glass in hand. The woman took a deep breath, surveyed the chaos, and then began a rapid muscular assault on it.

—You must be Professor Garner's char, said Miriam encouragingly.

The woman turned now and looked her up and down.

—I'm his daughter you know. From New York, said Miriam.

—I don't come in regular, said the woman, without showing any interest in the information. She already had all the dishes out of the breakfast room and into hot water.

—A pity, said Miriam plainly: When I was living here a few years ago this house was a home. You seem a capable woman. Perhaps I can persuade you to come in more often?

—It's too far out of hand, the woman muttered.

30

—I wouldn't mind paying you a little more than the going rate, pursued Miriam: I don't know what Professor Garner *is* paying, of course.

—No, I wouldn't want to work here regular, said the woman.

She rolled back the carpet, so that Miriam was forced to step rapidly on to the red tiling, as the woman gathered mop, plastic bucket and hot water in the same easy single movements. Under the mop tiles returned to the familiar clean surface. Miriam hesitated: When *do* you? Come in, I mean.

—I come in when Cressy goes off, said the woman: She calls me up and I come.

—Goes off? echoed Miriam, bewildered.

—Well, can you wonder at it?

—Are you a relation, asked Miriam slowly.

—I'm her aunt. Makes me sick, said the woman vehemently: Ought to be laws against it. You'd think she'd suffered enough, wouldn't you?

She looked more closely at Miriam now, taking in the fastidious clothes, white cuffs, and easy bearing.

—The house is too big for one girl to run, said Miriam.

But the woman was already in the scullery. Fresh suds smelled everywhere. The sink began to shine.

—Look at that stove, said Miriam: Could you do something to that?

The woman glanced at it.

—I can tell you what that wants doing to it, she said: Fumigating. I wonder she don't catch typhoid. That's encrusted, that is.

She opened the cupboard under the sink.

—No caustic, she said disgustedly.

—Look, said Miriam practically: Make me a list of what you need. A new head to that mop for one thing. Caustic soda you say. What else? I'll get it from the shops.

—Dirty old buzzard, muttered the woman.

—Well, look. If my father's confined to bed, reasoned Miriam: Obviously he needs a woman to help, doesn't he?

—Oh aye, he still needs a woman.

—Look Mrs – will you give your name? I'd like you to polish the hall. I'll buy Flash. And the polish? asked Miriam quietly: Can you?

—If I've time. It's not Mrs either, it's *Miss*. Miss Lyle.

—Miss Lyle, then, said Miriam: Since your niece doesn't feel responsible for anything so mundane as cleaning a floor, perhaps you can advise me where I *can* find help.

—Mundane? echoed the woman.

—Whatever she does for him, said Miriam slowly: It isn't the housework. That's all I mean. Agencies. There must be agencies.

The woman glowered: You'll not find many takers for the job, if you advertise she said: I mean, it's known. The house is *known*. Understand?

—Not yet, said Miriam, rather helplessly: My father is a Professor at the University. He's the Fellow of a College. If he's ill, he can make arrangements to move into College I'm sure. No-one would believe a man of his distinction could be living in such squalor.

Her voice faltered under Miss Lyle's sardonic eyes.

—We allus say University folk are the filthiest, she said: I worked as a Bedder once. You wouldn't believe what I've seen.

—You're thinking of undergraduates.

—They're men aren't they?

From upstairs a bellow of fury recalled Miriam to the glass she was carrying.

She found her father sitting up, with his teeth in, and glasses on.

—How could you leave me? Lying here. Can't you see I'm ill?

—Here's the water, said Miriam.

—Put it down then, he said querulously.

—But I thought you needed a drink? She held it out to him.

—I know when I want to drink, he said sulkily.

Miriam drew together the scattered forces of her spirit: Look, Dad, can I just ask? How did you manage before I arrived? I've only been here one night, you know. What did you do for someone to run errands when I wasn't here?

—How can you talk to me like that, he sighed: You're pitiless. I wouldn't treat a sick dog the way you treat me. What have you got for lunch?

—I'll go and see what there is, said Miriam steadily.

—But you haven't given it a thought, have you?

—There are eggs, I think, she said.

—Eggs! I'll turn into a chicken if I have any more eggs. What I need is a steak.

—If there is one, I'll fix it.

—*If*, he sighed: You see what I've come to. Well, at least light the fire. You'll find some matches by the window.

—Fire? But it's so hot in here already.

The old man peered at her.

—You've fattened a bit, he said: Suits you.

—Look, said Miriam: I will make you your food, always supposing I can find anything fit to eat in that muckheap downstairs, but when I come up again, this time there are one or two things you'd better get straight.

A crafty looked crossed her father's wizened mouth.

—More money?

—Money?

—Is that it?

—I'm not short of money, said Miriam flatly: Don't you understand I'm only here on a *visit*. Right? Of course I'm sorry to see you ill. But we'll have to arrange things differently. I've a lot of my own work to do, for one thing. And for another, I'm very bad at being ordered about.

—I don't mind paying *more* you know. To be comfortable.

—Are you deaf? I didn't *mention* money.

—No I'm not deaf.

—Well, you aren't *listening,* then, she said furiously.

Her father shut his eyes.

—I've one or two things to do, she said : Excuse me.

—Very well, very well, said her father huffily : As long as you aren't thinking of going out tonight.

Miriam gasped.

—Are you?

—Well, she said : Yes, as a matter of fact I've arranged to dine in Kings. With Jenny Hill, if you remember her.

—You'll just have to cancel it.

—*Why?* Miriam clutched at her head, and held on to her temper : Naturally I want to see a few colleagues, discuss plans. Precisely *why* can't I go out tonight?

—For one thing Stavros is coming round.

Miriam stared at her father incredulously.

—Are you out of your mind? He's in Los Angeles.

—Four months ago, perhaps. Now I come to think of it, his first letter did come from there. But once he was seriously involved, of course, he had to come over. He's been in Cambridge most of the term. Once he gets his teeth into something, he won't let up, will he? I admire that.

—But what can he have sunk his teeth into? Your *History of the Moors* for godsake?

—No need to sneer, said Garner coldly.

—It just seems so unlikely, said Miriam helplessly.

—When I first met him, I agree, I had certain unworthy suspicions myself. His persistent pouncing and ferreting has, perhaps, a certain sinister quality. I admit for a while I cheated a little and only fed him published material.

34

Until I understood the man's calibre. That white intensity marks the true scholar, the original mind, the enthusiast –

—Yes. But enthusiast for what? Whatever made him contact *you*? Garner shot his daughter an offended glare.

—He's a mathematician, she explained, undeterred : I'm sorry, it doesn't make sense to me.

—Then you don't know him as well as you think. Stavros is most interested in power.

Her father began to ruminate, almost to himself : And the instruments of power.

—You seem to have forgotten, said Miriam : that the Ptolomaic universe you know so much about doesn't work.

—Who mentioned Ptolomey? Daughter, I have made a discovery of such importance that it totally transcends history *or* science. I have found nothing less than the very point of time when Europe lost its soul; and the world fell into decay. Only this vile sickness prevents me presenting the world with a true vision.

—Visions? she said : Are you telling me Stavros is interested in visions? Look, Father, I *lived* with that man for two years, I doubt if he mentioned that. He may be a Fellow of your college but I reckon I know more about him than you do.

—Lived with him did you? No, I never knew that, her father said without much interest.

Such casual, indifferent tolerance unreasonably triggered near-hysteria in Miriam.

—You've invited him out of spite, she said : He's coming to *spite* me. That's what it amounts to.

Her father looked astonished : I don't know where you get such crazy ideas.

—Yes, yes, yes, she insisted : Don't pretend, and don't look at me like that. I know him.

35

—My head, he moaned : forgive me, I really can't *bear* arguments these days.

—Whenever could you? she shouted : You old fraud. I don't even *believe* you're ill. You must have some crafty *plan* in your mind, both of you.

The old man sighed : If you'd let me explain my plan as you call it perhaps you'd understand and be interested. Miriam could hear herself rising into incoherence : Explain Stavros? Here? With your connivance? How *dare* you arrange any meeting between us! You old fool. Did he tell you how we parted? Well – did he?

—We discussed symmetry, said her father quietly : Also snow crystals. Alhazen; the artist and mathematician as one. The light of heaven as manifest in cones and rays. Were *these* quarrels between you?

Miriam fought to hold down her fury : Of course not.

—Then you're behaving like a child, said her father : Very noisily.

But she was trembling all over; her handsome face and huge eyes fixed on the old man in a last effort to make him see the enormity of Stavros' presence. Under her hostile glare, however, her father only moaned a little, and reached for a towel to put on his head. Violently as she felt, Miriam noticed the towel was torn, and off-grey in colour, and wondered how he could bear to put his face into it.

—This is no use, she yelled : I'll leave you then.

His voice rose above hers : Rotten bitch. You and your rotten friends. Don't think they admire you. Why should they? What have you done that gives you the right to sneer at your poor old father? Blind, selfish generation! You'll all burn, you'll burn.

—Of course my friends know about me. So. We've more interesting things to talk about than your theories. They're good enough people. How *can* you curse them like that? Aren't you ashamed?

36

—My own daughter. How you talk to me. All you think about is food, drink, and the pleasures of your body!

He looked around him and sighed.

—Isn't there any fruit? he asked: Or a piece of cheese in the house?

Miriam walked boldly downstairs towards the conservatory, intending to stride straight out into the garden and confront the lazing Cressida in her deck chair; but instead, for a moment, the odours she had sensed before held her, and she sighed and paused, as an elusive half-memory presented itself to her almost as physically as a person. It was as if some delicate woman, with fine bones, and sad eyes, restrained her fever gently. As an inward memory, the vision faded almost at once; but the aura of some presence lingered; so that Miriam found herself in a half-trance, staring at the grey twigs of the peach tree, almost as if light had picked out the new vegetable green in it and bathed it with beauty.

And there she stood, incapable of movement; so still that even her hands paused in the sweep of her original gesture. Until the disturbance passed and she was able to frown and puzzle over the sense of broken time, even to shiver at the strangeness of the sensation. She was so totally unused to real illness; she had always taken the strength of a healthy animal for granted. The only things that had ever taken her to hospital had been broken limbs; or physical violence. Wasn't that so? And since then, good heavens, she had lived on the *certainty* of her own toughness. Could her body begin to fail her now?

Impatiently, she brushed the unwanted thought aside. Will and energy returned. Now she could, and did, stride out towards the deck chair, freshly determined to bring the girl back into sensible action. From behind she could still see the outline of a body in the deck chair.

But the experience in the conservatory had depressed her inwardly, and she was uneasily aware of some dream-like impediment slowing her usual rather haughty stride, so that it took longer than usual to cross the grass. Also there was something in the slant of the shadows from the clunch wall and the movement of sunshine in the yellow maple that disturbed her; perhaps more time had passed than she realized? The light at the extremity of each dancing mass of ochre leaves was an aureole of radiance only thrown by afternoon sun.

Her heart began to bang with a discomfort not far from fear; and yet she threw up her head angrily. And began to walk more firmly through the stubbly grass to confront the irritating girl. She rounded on the chair with her words ready and pungent, her limbs coursing with adrenalin.

But it was not Cressida sitting in the deck chair. And Miriam's voice died in her throat. Legs crossed, white-faced, blue eyes gleaming with malice : it was Stavros who met her angry stare with a polite smile. There he was, as he was etched on her memory, his jacket black velvet, his black hair pressed with unfashionable sleekness to his skull. His whole appearance marked by the same brutal purity, the same fanatic cleanliness of cut and feature.

—Well, now, Miriam, he said at once boldly : And what have *you* to say for yourself ?

3

—I'll have another of those, said Miriam : What's that, growing in the bottle?

—Herbs, said Jenny absently : It's just vodka. Shall I cancel Hall?

—No, why? Miriam stared : I don't seem to be explaining myself properly. Do I look drunk?

Her friend looked up from the other side of a circular table set with Victorian blue cups, Eccles cakes and Fitzbilly buns, all untouched, and smiled gently. Even in a tweed skirt, and plain jumper, with no colour on her face, she was a graceful woman.

—Well. You look a bit disturbed, she said.

—Disturbed? England, my God, England, said Miriam : Yes. You could say that. Jenny, *please* listen to me.

She tried again. Not only to describe the decay in the house; but her own helplessness in it, her sense of dwindling, of becoming invisible and inaudible; and even as she reported the sensations her own natural aplomb returned, so that, even to herself, the experience began to sound more like travel shock than metaphysics, and she ended up laughing.

—I give up. It's hopeless, sitting here. Everything is so *solid*. You are. With all your music in order, and plants everywhere. Lovely. Other people's homes always look solid. Sometimes I wish I could stop moving about all the time. When I see that street down there : all small shops with iron balconies and those spires in the sky, I do envy you! But I know it's a talent you have, for order and choice.

—I can't say I ever managed the same order and choice with Tim, said Jenny drily.

—How rude of me! I forgot – you're married, aren't you? Now.

—Well, said Jenny: I'm *not,* any more, so it doesn't matter. She looked as she spoke so completely whole and uncrabbed by loneliness that Miriam marvelled.

—You're extraordinary.

—No, honestly it was a very desperate mistake. He got really to hate me. When his friends came round he used to tell them everything.

—What everything?

—Well, how prim I was and Methodist, and how I liked to go to bed at ten. That sort of thing.

—I don't believe it.

—Well, I *do,* said Jenny seriously: Go to bed early.

—I mean Tim. Being so foul.

—No, it was my fault don't you see? I shouldn't have married him; I knew I wasn't going to enjoy it. I never *have* much liked men for sex, said Jenny: And gay women terrify me.

She began to clear the table.

—You mean you'd rather do it yourself? asked Miriam, appalled.

—If I get an overpowering urge, said Jenny: Why not? At least it always works. Don't you ever?

Miriam said: Good Lord, no.

Jenny raised her eyebrows sceptically.

—Well, all right, admitted Miriam: Maybe I do occasionally. But I've never heard anyone declare it was better than the real thing!

—Don't you think? said Jenny.

Miriam considered the matter.

—I mean *physiologically,* said Jenny: You don't get all

the spice of being admired and falling in love I realize, but that's something else, isn't it? Anyway, I've had some very intense dreams.

—Speaking physiologically?

—Quite.

—And Tim?

—Hopeless, said Jenny serenely : He could just never find the right place to rub.

Miriam was silent for a moment or two.

—I think I'll have another vodka, she said abruptly.

—What do you like best?

Miriam looked at the steady wrist filling the tumbler, and then up at her friend's small and earnest face.

—Sexually?

Jenny nodded.

—Are you getting some kind of kick out of this? demanded Miriam : Well I'm afraid I used to favour the straight screw if you want to know. Recently I suppose you could say I've been getting a bit kinky.

—And how was Stavros?

Miriam swallowed her vodka before replying.

—Stavros, she said then, rather huskily : He was *very* ingenious.

—Did I ever tell you? asked Jenny : I used to cross myself before going to supervisions with him.

—And when you got back? Don't bother to tell me.

—No, giggled Jenny : He was always too scary for that. And I like *beefy* men.

Miriam began to follow another line of thought : What the hell is he doing up there, humouring my father, who has clearly gone round the twist?

—He must be interested.

—But look. *You* do physics, don't you? What can you imagine using early Arabic computation for nowadays? Frankly? I mean there's no chance of it turning out to be useful or true is there?

41

—It could be useful without being true, said Jenny slowly.

Miriam said : You've lost me.

—It's like the square root of minus one.

—What?

—You remember. It doesn't exist, but you can't work the laws of physics without pretending it does.

—Oh dear, said Miriam : You're humouring *me* now.

Jenny laughed, and looked at her watch : Look, are you going to eat in Hall or not? She asked with a deprecating sideways tilt of her chin that Miriam remembered guiltily; it proclaimed how quickly she had yielded a kind of spiritual ascendancy to Miriam. For a moment Miriam wondered irritably why, with such bright black eyes and red, tender lips, Jenny chose such a quiet, self-effacing manner. And acknowledged that, left to herself, Jenny would have been happier talking about growing mint or the problems of the Elsan lavatory at her country cottage. They were corrupting each other with confessions. Miriam felt a sweet sick feeling she had almost forgotten, Jenny's docility encouraged a false flamboyance in her.

—Listen, she said, resisting the temptation to perform the anecdote : There's something else I forgot. Imagine this. I went back to my room after all that quarrelling, to pick up that scrawly school book; and then I remembered I'd hung up my best dress in the cupboard. So, god dammit, I crashed about in the dust among all the old rubbish in there, thinking it must have fallen down. Until suddenly I realized it had been *nicked*. It just *had* to be stolen. Can you imagine? And it cost a small fortune in Bloomingdales! So I strode over to my old room.

—Of course, Jenny agreed, raptly.

Miriam paused.

—Do sit up, she said impatiently : I'm trying to tell you what happened.

42

Miriam had marched across the landing and opened the door of her own old bedroom without ceremony. It was reassuringly clean, she observed, faintly scented, with the same warm geranium odour of her father's room but with open windows. The wardrobe was open too and empty, with the mirrored door hanging backwards.

—Oh!

A voice and a little rustle behind the door betrayed the presence of someone else in the room, presumably standing behind the wardrobe and looking into the mirror.

—Come out of there, said Miriam sharply : What are you doing?

—I've been cleaning up, said Cressida's voice hesitantly.

—Really? It will do very well as it is.

Cressida then came out from behind the mirror, and Miriam's hand went to her mouth; Cressida was wearing the missing dress. The effect was frighteningly unbecoming. The size was so far wrong that the shaping under the bust had collapsed completely; and hung like a comic dress on a dwarf. The sleeves hung over the edge of the narrow shoulders, so that the neckline had displaced itself to one side, and as Cressida hung her head in embarrassment, the bottom of the skirt lifted, and Miriam saw that she had tried to correct the skirt length with safety pins.

—Of all the bloody cheek!

—Well I liked it, said Cressida sullenly : Isn't it pretty? The colours.

—On you, it's hideous, said Miriam : Look, look at yourself.

—I could soon fix it, said the girl cunningly.

—Listen that's my dress, said Miriam : Take it off.

—No, said Cressida : I like it.

43

—Take it off, Miriam had screamed, with a sense of all her authority going from her like blood seeping away.

Cressida hesitated : Rotten bully, she said, defiantly.

—Look, said Miriam, grasping at patience as if she were dealing with a small child : I don't want to have to make you take it off by force. It would only tear. But it is *my* dress. I want it. Understand?

But did she any more? Want it? Distorted over the grotesque angularity of Cressida's body, Miriam could hardly remember how the cloth had looked on her own full body. She felt a sudden disgust at the thought of wearing it, with the parody of this misshapen form inside it, pulling it out of shape.

—It looks absurd on you, she said weakly.

—I'll alter it, I'm good with a needle, said Cressida sensing an advantage.

—Oh for godsake, said Miriam : Do what you like. Are all your things out of here?

—Yes.

—Good.

Cressida's face lit up suddenly with childish delight : You're so beautiful. I wish.

—What? said Miriam impatiently, turning her back on her own decision.

—We could be like sisters. Could we? You could teach me.

—My god, I've enough to do here as it is, said Miriam : Teach you what anyway?

—What *they* do. You know. With the books. You can read them, can't you?

—Who are you talking about?

—You can read Arabic, can't you?

—You want to learn Arabic? echoed Miriam : But why?

The girl took off the dress now, under Miriam's eyes without selfconsciousness. Miriam was astonished. She

44

had almost no breasts at all, and the line of her ribs was clearly visible.

—Don't you get enough to eat? she asked abruptly.

—Yes. It's only hormones, Dr Garner. That's what keeps me so thin. I could have an operation on my thyroid only –

One shoulder went up in a shrug.

—I'm scared, you see. That's it. There's something bad written for me this year. It's in those books. That's why I want to know. *They* never tell me anything.

—Put some clothes on, said Miriam firmly: You're shivering. Cressida, there can't be anything in those books about *you*. They're old books; full of prophecies that never came true. *Ever.*

—Ah, but they didn't have the maths for it then, said Cressida sagely: They got all the dates wrong.

—I'll *look* at them for you, said Miriam slowly: If you'll tell me who's been feeding you this nonsense? And why? Cressida dropped her head and said nothing.

—Who are *they*? demanded Miriam.

—Why, your dad of course. And his friend.

—They're mocking you.

—No. Sometimes they let me help, like I said. Only they never tell me everything. I know we're going to stop the fall of Europe; they *said* that. Only *then,* not now. *Halt* it, you see. But something has to happen to me first.

—I never heard such a load of shit, said Miriam roughly.

—Well, said Jenny: That's straightforward enough, anyway.

—Not to me. How do you mean?

—I mean it's shit, like you said. Look, if we're going to Hall, we should *go*. Do you want to?

—Yes, why not? Miriam betrayed a certain relief: Except I haven't a gown, does it matter?

45

—Not here. It's informal.

—Still I *wish* I had put on something gaudier.

—I've got some jewellery, suggested Jenny tentatively:
Well, I don't know what *you'll* think of it. My parents
brought it back from Jerusalem, along with the most
extraordinary little bags of coloured sand, and Jordan
water. Honestly! But the necklace. Well, you have a
look.

She went to a bureau, unlocked it carefully, brought
out a box with white tissue inside, and unwrapped the
necklace. Miriam stared at it: It's real, she said.

—Real *what,* though?

—Silver, probably Berber not Yemenite; with *azulejo*
work. *Why* don't you like it?

Jenny held it up against her woolly jumper: Look.

—It's beautiful.

—It is, but be honest, now, Miriam. Have I the *style* for
it?

—Just a minute. I'll have to open the neck of my
blouse. There. Wow, said Miriam: Can I really borrow it?

—Of course. And you'd better stay the night here. What
do you think?

—It's a good idea. I could go back after coffee to get the
rest of my stuff, couldn't I?

—Must you? said Jenny, practically: Have you got a
key? How will you get back *into* the house? Shouldn't
you phone, and leave the whole question of collecting
things till tomorrow?

—Can't phone. It's off the hook, said Miriam. She
whirled round: But I'll climb in if I have to. It's hardly
New York round here.

—I wish you wouldn't go back, late at night, said Jenny:
I know it's nonsense. All the same.

—Well, I'm not leaving that mad bitch *all* my clothes,
said Miriam, intricately adjusting her neckline: Anyway
there's Dad.

—You aren't worried about him?

—Yes, of course, said Miriam impatiently: Didn't I say so? I'll have to talk to the doctor. Find out what's really wrong with him. Meanwhile, tell me – who'll be dining tonight?

—It's out of term, you know, said Jenny, apologetically: Most of the fellows you'd remember are away.

—All right, who's new?

—Well, there's a rather handsome Sufi.

—What fun, said Miriam: I'll try out my Koran.

—Hm. Don't be disappointed. He's probably from London. Anyway, his English is good. An American or two. One Jap.

—Let's go, said Miriam.

They hurried down a heated corridor of glass, down a long staircase out into the September evening. The air was soft and warm; which made it possible for Miriam to pause and stare up at the grey buttresses, and look back at the long stretch of grass falling down to the river. It was not that the new building obtruded, only that the long corridors had in some way diminished a space that in her memory had been enormous. Plants would cover the new buildings also; but the glass would remain. The new stones had been correctly chosen to match the grey stones of earlier ages. They were unyielding, utterly East Anglian in their bleakness; even Druidical. Other colleges had used warmer stones; so the builders of this ancient place had chosen thoughtfully; only the Victorian court was yellow; only that caught the last rays of the sun into itself as stone could.

—North European Gothic, Miriam said: What a brutal form it was. And how absolutely right also, that the glories of such an age should look as they do.

—Don't you remember the glass inside? said Jenny, rather hurt: You aren't supposed to judge it from out here.

47

—Yes of course. And the fan roofing soars, I remember.
—Do move on, though. We'll have missed sherry (which may be just as well) but we don't want to miss the whole meal, do we?

A gentleman with grey hair and a jacket of a similar salt and pepper speckle came up to them both, and they all three quickened their steps towards the Hall. For different reasons, the gentleman and Miriam fell behind.
—Are you a wife? he asked her, with breathly abruptness as they paused together at the door of the dining hall.
—A *wife*? Miriam was genuinely puzzled: No.

By oak walls, under the gilt-framed, faintly-surprised faces of seventeenth-century gentlemen and Victorian burgesses in full red robes, a number of the younger fellows and their guests sat, eating melon or white fish. Miriam waved vaguely at a woman who was staring across at her with evident recognition; but allowed herself to be steered away in another direction under Jenny's hissed warning.

The silver shone on the wood; the oak table had been set for another dozen or so; there were no lights in the lower part of the hall. Nevertheless, an age-old sense of privilege, not so much a matter of free food, and good food, nor even the deference of college servants; but the sense of *belonging* that certain dining clubs must have given to men, once, when England was rich, still hung everywhere here. The privilege was shared by a casual collection of fellows and guests who began to surround her. Two biochemists, one from New York, introduced themselves across the table. Another man, with a blue oblong plastic disc on his lapel and a long face, looked as if he had possibly lost his own conference. Miriam checked that his gloom did not rise from some simple language barrier; but he was, it turned out, a Chilean, and his thoughts

48

were wholly elsewhere, with his family in South America.

Rather as Miriam had feared, her sad, grey-haired running companion took the seat next to her, as if they were old friends. Then a middle-aged man of round-faced benevolence took the remaining outlet; and Miriam settled gloomily into sobriety.

—Did you see in *The Times* today, the newcomer began, however, at once: Old Age Pensioners have got a magnificent racket. They've been selling their barbiturates at so much a pill in the teenage drug scene. How about *that* for beating inflation? My name is Sidney, he said simply.

—Don't read the newspapers, responded Miriam's other neighbour.

—No time? asked Miriam.

—They rot your head, m'dear, newspapers. Liberal cant, all of them.

—Not sure I'd call *The Times* liberal, said Miriam doubtfully.

—Take my word for it. All the same names. Look and see. Weeklies. Sundays. All the same bunch. Wet, limp, and dangerous.

—You have to understand what's happening in England now, said Sidney in her ear: We think we may have a revolution on our hands. I don't think they've noticed in America.

—Well, the economic crisis, said Miriam: I suppose. Or do you mean the I.R.A.? Bombers and so on?

—Nothing like that. It's moral collapse, said Sidney in a low voice.

—What's *his* subject? Is he an economist? Miriam whispered.

—Good God no, that's Dr Pringle, said Sidney: Our economists are all *left*-wing. Pringle's a historian. Are you doing a Ph.D.?

His small, hot eyes ran over her face and neck as he

spoke. She knew exactly what he was really asking.

—Sorry. All done years ago. And I'm not a wife, she said hastily : Jenny brought me in.

—Oh yes, that's right. You're her Arabist. Do you know London?

—I was born there, said Miriam : Why?

—The areas that used to be Jewish ghettos have filled up with Pakistanis. So the Synagogues all over the East End are turning into Mosques. Don't you find that rather poetic?

—My goodness, she said, realizing : *You* must be Jenny's Sufi. I'm sorry, I just took for granted you'd be coloured. English you know, but — what got you on to it?

—I was in Jerusalem. On a sabbatical. I suppose it made more sense over there, he said credibly : I think it was just a way of asserting the visionary possibility in man without having to take in all that Christian bullshit.

—What about *Moslem* bullshit? I have the impression that's quite hard to shake off in its own way.

—Ah, but I didn't inherit that, he said smiling : So it's easier.

—I know who you are, said Pringle suddenly : You're *Garner's* daughter. Better mannered, but you *look* like him.

—Thank you, said Miriam dubiously.

—Utterly wrong, mark you. Absolutely ignored the Latin tradition of scribes and monastic transmission.

—No he didn't, said Miriam : I thought this had all been fought over long ago. The Christians didn't even have the *books* until later, did they? Think of the *luck* of a Moslem like Avicenna. There he was, with a whole library of Aristotle, Greek medicine and mathematics round him in Bukhara; and what did the Christian West have? A few poets, the church fathers and Latin school-masters. What's more they didn't always let in the *poets*. Think of St Odo on Virgil.

50

Miriam became aware that the two biochemists across the table from her had been stopped cold in mid flow by this exchange.

—Do I gather you are an *Arabist*? the American asked. Both biochemists were Jewish, she now decided; and together they looked across waiting for her answer as if it had political weight.

—Medieval historian of, she said, lightly : Yes. Moorish Spain, mainly.

The Americans did not immediately turn back to one another and their discussion of T-cells and gamma-globulin, however.

The grizzled American bent forward : My name is Saul Gershon. Surely you are speaking with some prejudice? Don't you think, Miss?

—No, said Miriam equably : None at all. In the black Ages I'm talking about, most Greek knowledge had been lost to Europe, and only translation from Arabic into the Romance languages made the Renaissance possible.

—And the beginnings of scientific thought, said Sidney.

—Look here, said Pringle, doggedly bypassing Gershon : Young lady. Your father was never fair to the Church. Never had any sense of the Saracens as a real threat. All this gentle tolerance he parades so elegantly is much less than half the story, you know.

—At least it is on record, said Miriam drily : The tolerance, I mean; I'm not denying the occasional massacre. But take the treatment of the Jews as an index. Pringle glared : Why?

Miriam said patiently : Because they were useful people. Islam could use them. The Church tormented them down the centuries.

—No doubt. I've often thought, said Pringle heavily : Without Christian faith, it's quite impossible to understand medieval history. Why can't you see the survival of the whole Church was at stake? There *were* pagans on the North of us too, you know. I hope you don't hold some insane brief for their cultural genius?

—Just a minute, broke in Gershon.

Pringle turned a ferocious single eye sideways upon him: You aren't a *Finn,* I hope?

Gershon laughed, without self-deprecation, and without diffidence. Miriam warmed to him.

—No, my family came from Odessa. Through Vilna. We're Jews.

—I see, said Pringle, non-committally.

Miriam remembered Pringle now. Her father had described him once as a 'gleeful bigot'. And certainly he seemed to be enjoying the possibility of some neat snub that could be smartly administered.

—I was just wondering, said Gershon: What makes you feel the Church deserved so much protection? Any more than the Mafia? I mean, it was hardly the repository of humane values was it? And it put down almost *every* truth *I* was taught at school through its entire history.

—The most generous comment is to hope your school was at fault; the Church was the repository of the single most important truth the world has ever been vouchsafed, growled Pringle.

Gershon said: Are you open to argument on that?

The college servants in their white coats crossed the truculence in the air with their silver platters of roast beef, asparagus, and small roast potatoes, while Miriam's heart sank.

—Not on that, she said quickly: You'd be wasting your time.

—I've got time, Gershon said.

Pringle looked pointedly at his wrist.

At which moment Miriam became aware of Jenny at her shoulder, sensitive to the tempo of the discussion, and interfering quickly and clumsily: It's the conflict of so many *rights,* isn't it? That's what makes the history of Europe *so* tragic. Can I take the spare seat?

For the first time Miriam felt the gulf that had opened up and separated her now from Cambridge as if Pringle and Jenny belonged to a smugly righteous village into which both Gershon and she had blundered. Outside, blood might dry in the sand; but issues would always be settled by candlelight and quietly in this chill hall. She could feel Gershon's anger growing with his sense of enveloping cottonwool as Jenny's voice, designed to soothe him, with every cadence put him into his place. For a moment Miriam remembered with pleasure her father's reputation for rudeness. At least he would never be just chatting along like Jenny or bothering with a topic that was just an *issue*; something to be picked up and sent across the table a few times like a social game in which it was almost a rule that there wasn't going to be any fundamental change in *thought.* Miriam remembered New York. She recalled London. Was such remoteness *possible* among intelligent people anywhere else but in this dim, candle-lit hall, these safely cosseted creatures? Her heart sank. It was a cold, passionless countryside.

—Well, and I'm not sure I believe *you* altogether, Dr Garner, said Gershon.

Miriam started guiltily.

—I'm sorry. What did you say?

—What about the poor Jews in Iraq? asked Dr Gershon: Aside from which, I happen to have *seen* North Africa, and if that is what you mean by living alongside one another Dr Garner.

—Politics have changed things, I know. But Moslems and Jews prayed *together* once. Have you seen Hebron? she said: I was thinking of centuries ago.

—And did you know, said Sidney: that the Arabs tell legends that are also in the Talmud?

Miriam drank down her glass of wine and regretted

53

the whole turn of the discussion. Her stomach felt sour and she would have preferred to be alert. Also the dazzle of candle and silver together was disturbing. She refused the Crème Caramel; and as soon as the coffee came, she began to suck eagerly on a cigarette. Meanwhile Sidney's soft voice went on and on, and the sharp, New York face turned towards him and listened.

—There was once an old Berber woman, he was saying: and she believed in the Moslem law. When the Jews wanted to gather the bones of their dead and depart she told them, if you want the bones of Joseph, come with me, I will show you where they are. They are buried under the Tagus, where the water flows deeper than it did when you people came first. When the water falls, you will find a sarcophagus. Right?

Miriam patted her head with a white tissue from in her handbag.

—I've heard that story before, she said, muzzily: But surely it was told of the Nile? To Moses?

—There are many stories, said the biochemist emphatically: What about a few facts? It's the facts get muddled up, not bones. Who cares about bones?

—Jenny, I think I'd better go, Miriam said: If I'm going to collect my things. I'll get a taxi.

—Aren't you staying for port?

—No, it's nine now. You know, by the time I get out to my father's house, it'll be late enough.

—I suppose that's sensible, said Jenny: Though I can easily lend you something to sleep in. You can collect your stuff in the morning, really.

—I'm sorry, I feel stubborn about it, said Miriam smiling.

—I'll walk you to the Porter's lodge.

The one thing Miriam hadn't expected was her father awake, dressed and furious with worry. He answered the first ring of the doorbell, and pulled her roughly inside the hallway.

—Why are you *up*? Miriam asked, freeing herself and staring at him. He had washed and shaved, and looked altogether in physical control.

—*Why?* What kind of a father do you think I am? Off you go, like a bolt of lightning, without a word about where or even who you're going to see. What do you expect?

—If you'll just cast your mind back, said Miriam: We parted on rather bad terms.

—Does that mean you can't give a thought to an old man's heart? You have no feelings. None.

—Dad, that's not true, said Miriam, weakened by the tone of concern: But, goddamnit, I've lived away from home a long time. You get out of the habit of *saying* where you're off to. Nobody cares.

She started up the stairs, determined to collect her cases nevertheless.

—Are you going to bed? he asked: I've some tea made in the kitchen.

She paused then, with her hand on the stairs, and looked back at him, with pain. He made so touching a figure; just standing there, hopefully.

—That *was* kind, she said weakly.

—It's early, he said: We could have a proper talk.

—Dad, I *can't* stop now, she said, with a pang of guilt: I've got a cab outside. You know, I've just come back to collect my clothes.

—You mean you aren't *staying* with me? He seemed stupefied.

—Dad, I'll come in and see you tomorrow. Honestly. There's a lot I want to know. About your work, she lied rapidly: I'd *like* to help.

—Yes, and you can, he said eagerly: I'll send away the cab, shall I?

—No, she insisted, on a shriller note : I promised Jenny. Don't worry. I'll come back here in the morning, though.

He began to follow her up the wide staircase, quite nimbly.

—At least don't go *up* yet.

His unexpected turn of speed increased her own, until she was almost running across the landing towards her bedroom.

—Miriam, Miriam, please ! Listen to an old man ! You *mustn't* go in there. Not *now,* please.

In spite of herself, Miriam paused for a moment with her hand on the door-handle.

—Wait, he panted, following close behind.

Miriam flung open the door with desperate resolution.

For a moment she stood in the doorway, looking about in the room which was already lit, though faintly. Across the bed lay Cressida asleep. She was quite naked. As Miriam watched, the white figure of a man approached the bed. He approached slowly and deliberately and without excitement; by his gait alone she would have recognized him. It was Stavros. His face was without expression, but she could see that his penis was fully extended in a monstrous erection.

The girl on the bed did not move. She was surely unconscious; no sleep could have been so deep. Stavros leant over her. Very quietly he parted her legs and extended each in a diagonal, for ease of penetration. Miriam could see the surprisingly heavy hair, and the female orifice lying between purple folds of flesh. She leant back against the doorpost, her own breath quickening, her own sexual juices beginning to flow against her will.

Still without showing any interest in the girl below him, Stavros knelt quietly over her body, so that the tip of his penis touched the entrance to her body; then, slowly he began to lower himself into her.

Miriam gasped, and the noise made him turn a blank bemused look in her direction. Their eyes met. At once he leant backwards and pushed himself swiftly and fully into the sleeping girl; his eyes fixed on Miriam's. Miriam knew he had let himself ejaculate with the pleasure of feeling her eyes on him. She was angry. And yet against her will, a horribly strong sexual pleasure swept her from between her legs to the veins in her wrist.

Then there was the click of an electrical switch and the whole room began to flicker with strobe lighting. The furniture was no longer continuous. The four walls of the room had broken open. The world was nothing but a succession of flashes and darkness, in which frame by frame Stavros was approaching. In the first his skin was radiant and she saw his thin mouth stretched over his teeth. Then with a jerk he was blackness. In the next frame, she saw his genitals glow blue. Then he was blackness itself. Until he was erect standing over her in a blaze of light.

4

—She isn't crying out, is she?
—No. She's in some kind of continuous orgasm.
—Stavros, are you *sure* we ought to call a doctor? It's hardly a medical matter, is it?
—Why don't you come and look?

Astonishing, the smallest stretch, the movement of a toe, and *there*. Again. Soaring. Sweetly. *Every* time. Upwards. Thoughts scattering. Back. Through the seasons. Red leaves, apple blossom, first green shoots. Brown crunch of underfoot leaves; then wet leaves; rain and there! It was so easy. Hot sun. *Higher*.

Into Summer, Summer, Summer. . . .

—Be careful.
—Just put this blanket over her.
—Get the mouthpiece in.
—*Must* you? Do all that?
—We *have* to tie her arms, guv'nor. Get her down the stairs.
—No, let me talk to her.
—If she can hear you.

Through silence, over white sands beyond granite hills there! The city is an island. How to drop down on to an

island of rough banks. Gorges. Cliffs falling into the
water; into water, or wilderness of rock. Quietly. And
quickly, before it is evening; how fast the light goes; over
white sand, and low houses, white on whitened sands :
outside the city. Moonlight. No-one is moving. The doors
and windows are shut. The sand covers the streets.
Everywhere is silent; it's like passing over a cemetery;
over houses of the dead, and mosques of the dead. And
these houses have no tenants. This is the desert of the
dead with nothing but the moon like a sliver of grey
mother-of-pearl in the sky. . . .

—Why have you got her wired up like that? I want to
know.
—*Please* just fill in this form, it's only routine, said the
houseman weakly.
—You could answer a simple question, couldn't you?
—Has your daughter any history of epilepsy? *Petit mal*?
—Absolutely nothing of the kind.
Stavros took his arm and led him to one side saying
gently : Surely you must realize what's happened?
Octavius Garner stared with hostility at him : Cressida's
asleep in bed like a cow, as usual. Isn't she?
Stavros shrugged : I suppose so. Leave this to me. I'll fill
in the form.

The falling has stopped but the city continues. It has
streets, arches, other inhabitants, mealtimes, weather.
It has time. The skies change. There are other inhabitants.
Donkeys as well as people. Flies. The *Calle de Morro*. A
great house. Inlaid wood on the doors; a frieze of plaster-
work. Inside : geraniums, ceramic pots. Servants in silk.
She has been given a saffron-coloured dress. She is
in a family house. And this morning, Miriam is taking
coffee with Ibn Ezra.

Thickset and short limbed, with black hair, and blue eyes fixed on Miriam's face, Ibn Ezra sat in his garden, nodding : *Al Bayt baytak,* he said, and motioned her to take one of the small cakes that lay on a plate between them. They were sitting together under an apricot tree. Around the garden was a walk of Mudejar arches; sheltered from the sun were pools of water, and miraculous vegetation; cherries, almonds, citrus trees. Lillies grew in the waters. There was a geometric pattern of blue and white ceramic tiles on the wall behind them.

The cake tasted of ground almond and egg yolk. Miriam ate it, and said nothing.

Ibn Ezra squinted sideways at her slyly : So you came out of the desert? In that necklace? Did you? Listen, I am an old man but I am not a fool.

Miriam looked upwards. Above the arches were wooden galleries. Along one of them, she caught a sudden glimpse of women, dressed in fine colours, with sashes and girdles glinting with gems.

—That one is my daughter, said Ibn Ezra, putting another cake in his mouth, and speaking through the crumbs : She has my nose, poor girl; and her eyes are unfortunately even more Asiatic. May I tell you about my son-in-law?

Before Miriam could reply, a terrible wailing cry, as if of a young child in great pain, came from an upstairs room. Hastily, the shutters were drawn; but the cry, muted though it was, rose higher and higher.

—In God's name, what was that? asked Miriam.

—Luis' child is ill, said Ibn Ezra, with apparent indifference : He is a pampered sickly boy. Two days ago he cut his foot on a stone, and now he lies as if he had been poisoned by a scorpion. Let us continue our conversation a little.

Miriam said nothing.

—I want to welcome you to the land of the *Sefarad,* said

60

Ibn Ezra: Our people here are an ancient flower; we were exiled by Nebuchadnezzar, long before Christ. Therefore we are untouched with his blood; which some say is the cause of our good fortune. Certainly, we have been lucky.

Miriam said: So I see.

Ibn Ezra frowned at her tone: Perhaps you think us lax? Because we cultivate a good life?

Miriam said: I think you have been lucky.

Ibn Ezra continued to muse aloud without taking his eyes from her face: Luis told me about your companions, especially the red-haired one. Those red hairs, my dear, have a tradition. The Moslems say that when Moses had pounded the golden calf to dust, he made the Israelites who had sinned drink the water. Did you know that? In this way certain Jews became red-haired, and they transmitted the sign of their sin to their posterity.

—If you believe that, said Miriam: You will believe anything.

—They were Hebrews. Why should they run from Toledo? asked Ibn Ezra: We have a King here who calls himself Ruler of the Three Religions. Our synagogues are beautiful as mosques. It is a true description. Here there are Jewish *farmers*, as well as tailors and weavers. We can buy and sell any goods we think of. We even have our own guilds. Here we can be whatever we choose: silversmiths, saddlers, basketmakers, or scholars. Where else in Europe will you find that? And we can live in great houses. This house was bought by my son-in-law's family from a Moor a hundred and fifty years ago. Where else will you find a hundred and fifty years of a single Hebrew family in a single house?

Another great cry rose from the shuttered room upstairs but this time, Miriam only dropped her eyes, sullenly.

—Do you think *I* want to be here? She asked.

—Where do you want to be? In Narbonne? The Jews of Narbonne once scoured the world for jewels for Abd-al-Rahman; but their situation now is less happy. Have you heard? Your story does not please me, said Ibn Ezra : You say you have not been in this city before, and your tongue is certainly strange. Perhaps you will allow me to tell you another story?

—You *think* in stories, said Miriam : It seems to me!

—It is my tradition, said Ibn Ezra.

Miriam shrugged, and the cold blue eyes of her crafty questioner took in the masculine gesture with interest, even as he began to speak : It is a story from Granada, from the time when concubines from the North were highly prized. They say a rich purchaser brought a girl home with him once; all the way from the North on a mule; and they spoke little on the way, because he could not understand her language. Then as he drew near to his own house, a scabrous maker of bird cages yelled some insult at the girl; of such a nature she at once lost her temper and replied as filthily in the language of Granada. So the rich man was soundly tricked; though I do believe he sold the girl afterwards for a profit.

—I don't want to be any man's concubine; said Miriam angrily : I'd prefer to be out of your stories and fantasies.

She stood up rudely. And was walking off, when the cry from the child upstairs was heard again; this time, it was a single shrill note, falling to a whimper. Miriam put her hands to her ears.

—He is being treated now, said Ibn Ezra : The doctor is with him. Don't be so squeamish. The child will be dead in a week.

—I want to see him, said Miriam harshly : Order your doctor to let me in to him. Perhaps I can help.

—Listen, said Ibn Ezra quietly : The physician is a Christian. What can he do? He knows no astrology, and he cannot even read Galen. I think my daughter has called her Christian doctor, because her heart is wandering. He is a priest; uneducated, dangerous. I am humouring her; she is my daughter. But I'm warning you; to be *conversa* is to fall out of my protection altogether.

—Poor girl, said Miriam : To be drawn that way she must be bitterly unhappy.

—She is mad! It is her ugliness drives her, cried Ibn Ezra : Do you know that poverty is inevitable, that all the possessions of a *conversa* fall into the royal treasury?

—Is that what disturbs you? asked Miriam coldly.

—When we go upstairs, said Ibn Ezra : Look out of the window. You will see many women in black clothes carrying home their herbs and poor food, and their faces will look lined and old and full of spite. They are not Moslem women who come into market with their donkeys and walk with proud heads. They are Christian women; Mozarabes. The Arabs left them alone, but now they are uncertain. The priests from the North worry them. And so they are ugly; old before their time. It was from your face I knew you were no Christian.

—Women who are poor always age fast, Ibn Ezra, said Miriam : As you well know, if you believe in the light of reason, as I do.

—Do you believe fanatically? he said, with a certain unease : in this light?

—No, Miriam reassured him : I believe with Aristotle and the Greeks. Most moderately.

Ibn Ezra stood and looked at her with sudden slant eyes. For the first time she realized just how short he was.

—And in what language have you read him?

—In your words, she said serenely.

—More of this, later, he said.

As they walked inside, he pointed out with pride the iridescent mauve glaze on the tiles within the house, and the beauty of the ornately scripted patterns.

—The Moors are for ever the best artisans, he said :

They make the finest gardens. How well they build and how magnificent is their style of life; even the Christians will come to savour it.

He pointed to the plain white canted pillars and arches beyond, to the intricate carvings, with pinecones and strapwork, all the grace of proportion and space that filled him with joy.

—The Christian North is a desert, said Ibn Ezra: We civilize people here.

He paused.

—This is the child's room. When you have seen him, come and tell me what you think.

He opened the door for her.

The child lay on many cushions and rugs, in dim light. His huge eyes were glazed, and saw nothing; occasionally his body jerked. He plainly had a high fever.

The physician watched her entry with deep suspicion. She saw two things at once. His hands were washed, and his robe was Frankish. Nevertheless she spoke to him in Arabic calmly: How have you dressed the wound?

—The wound is small, lady. Still I have put mud from the Tagus, mixed with Cinnabar upon it. You see it will not draw.

—Show me.

The inflammation of the leg was impossible to miss; but she saw with relief that the redness was still local. She felt in the boy's groin; the nodes were only a little swollen; the wound's infection had not yet run far.

She said: Bring me soap. And good running water.

The physician muttered: Do you want to scent a corpse?

—Soap, she repeated: *Any* soap. Send to the market. The Arab stalls will be best. And also bring me *arak*.

He stared: Do you want the child to leave this world drunken to a stupor?

64

—Perhaps you have some other alcohol? I don't mean wine. Do not ask your master, she said, thinking quickly : Ask Luis' wife, the boy's mother. She will give you money. In any case she is paying you is she not?

The droop of an eyelid perhaps confirmed as much.

—Tell her, she whispered : Her son will live. Then she will give you money readily.

—I am here for the boy's soul, muttered the priest : I dare not promise more.

—Then promise nothing said Miriam : Get me running water and soap. Good water, remember that.

The wound was small, a flap of skin like the triangle produced by a broken blister. The child moaned, as the mud was washed off, and the unhealthy flesh released its yellow pus. Miriam pressed the wound, and the child moaned again. Impatiently she washed it away and the liquid formed again. And again.

—You see, said the physician.

—The body has its own defences, she said queerly : But the injury must be clean. Show me the stone on which the boy cut himself.

As she suspected, the stone had been preserved. She examined it.

—It was from running water?

—The Tagus.

—Where do your sewers empty? Answer, she said impatiently : Above or below where the boy was playing?

—Downstream.

—Hold his arms, she said : This will hurt horribly. I wish I could explain to the child.

Then she pressed the cruel, harsh alcohol undiluted into the wound. The boy cried out, and appeared to lose consciousness.

—*Now.* If you want my protection, put *nothing* on the wound. No mud. No Cinnabar. No gold dust.

—I will do as you say, bowed the priest.

—Put cold towels to his head, she said : Bring down his fever. Don't be afraid.

—Are you also a believer? the priest asked quickly in an undertone.

She met his eyes. Underneath the priestly stoop, and the unwashed smell was something familiar; a thin, wiry body. When he lifted his eyes for the first time to meet hers they were a blue of a Northern chill very different from Ibn Ezra.

—You are not Mozarabe? she said uncertainly.

—No. I follow the Latin rite. It is the true Church, he whispered : We shall conquer.

Miriam backed away.

There were two black teeth in his sly smile, but it was the ingratiating complicity that alarmed her. Instinctively she knew that she had pleased him; not because he thought the child would be helped by her treatment, but on the contrary because he thought it would be harmful. He clearly assumed they were acting under the same, secret directive. But to whom could the child's death be an advantage?

She looked at the child's pale face, broad-nosed with lines running from nose to mouth like an undernourished baby; he was certainly under-sized for five years. Also he had a fist thrust against his mouth to hold it open, as a baby might; and she could see his small milk teeth, which were perfect as seeds. He stirred, and moaned again; and then suddenly opened his black eyes wide on Miriam's face. Seeing her, his face cleared, and he said something sleepily which she could not catch.

—You see, the priest said raptly : He thinks himself already with an angel of Christ in heaven.

Miriam frowned.

—Pardon, said the priest.

—You spoke without thinking, said Miriam softly : You

66

must have been watching too long. Send for one of the servants of Ibn Ezra's daughter to take your place here. He seemed to understand immediately: You are right. The Church must have clean hands.

—*Ecclesia abhorret sanguinem,* said Miriam with irony: Exactly. So you'd better get some rest.

When the priest had gone, she paced about the room. kicking at the aromatic rushes, and trying to place the smell. Rosemary? Coriander? Where had she, once before, long lost, smelled the same sweetness, pressed into linen? In what wooden chest, in what locked door of her memory? She watched the child turn again in his sleep; and was just preparing to wet a cloth again for his temples, when she became aware of angry voices. The priest had left the door open slightly, and she moved towards it, intending to shut out the sounds of quarrelling from the sleeping child. A huge turquoise falcon, a ceramic of Persian design, stood on the lintel; for a moment she hesitated to move the object; and then the conversation itself caught her attention. She could see neither speaker. One voice was masculine, young and arrogant; the other, nasal and distressed. Miriam knew she was listening to the boy's mother.

—Luis, remember he is an old man. Please.

—Is this my house? Or his?

—You know it's yours. No-one questions that.

—But you *do* question it. Every day. In your behaviour. Because Ramon is *my* friend, isn't he?

Miriam could not catch the next sentences, since they were punctuated with the woman's tears.

—Am I talking unreasonably? Cruelly?

—No.

—Then for Godsake stop snivelling!

—You don't understand, she cried out: My father *fears*

Ramon. How can I over-rule him? Must Ramon come to supper tonight?

—So you agree with him? How very unsurprising. I wish I understood just how he has worked himself into the authority he enjoys here. You do whatever he wants; you do anything he asks. In the name of peace, you say.

—For peace, yes. We must have peace, Luis.

—Peace! On *his* terms, you mean. It's abject, pitiable. I'm ashamed.

—Are you? And he condemns me as a disobedient child! Oh it's hopeless, neither of you understand me. You don't even want to. You're both so busy making sure no-one pushes you one inch off course, why do I try so hard to please both of you? I could die and no-one would care, no-one.

—You have no dignity, Luis muttered: I suppose it must be hard for a plain woman. And worse for one without a dowry.

—Oh my god, must you remind me of that again?

—It explains a great deal.

—It has nothing to do with Ramon coming here tonight.

—It has everything to do with the way you crawl about, terrified to give orders to your own servants. Don't you understand that's what I'm objecting to? Your spineless pliancy.

—Yesterday you called me stubborn.

—You're stubborn enough to fight me. When you're afraid for your peace. And you're always afraid, aren't you? Of what *he* may say to hurt you.

—Why do you always make me sound so feeble? I'm trying to be dutiful, to honour my father. Isn't that right?

—A woman should honour her husband also.

—I do honour you, Luis.

—Do you? Then go in now and tell that old bully we are having friends. Tonight. Tell him not to worry. They are not *conversos*.

68

—And shall I invite him to dine with us?
—No.

Both voices dropped; and with a start of guilt, Miriam realized the intensity of her attention. The quarrel had an uneasy resonance, like something remembered from childhood. For the length of it, she had even forgotten the sick boy and her fears for him. At the same time it occurred to her, that it was strange; to have a child lying so ill, and have no-one even mention the illness. Could it be they did not care, or did not know his danger?

She sank on to a pile of rugs, suddenly giddy; as if the solidity of the whole edifice round her were shaken by some other reality, even with the thought of her own childhood.

—Father?
—Yes. What can I do for you?
—Do?
—Do you want something?

Miriam realized she had slept a while and was once again an inadvertent listener.

—Why have you so little *spirit*? demanded Ibn Ezra: Women should understand how to manage husbands.

—I loathe that word 'managing'; you talk as if women should be skilled like prostitutes.

—No. But Islam understands women well. They *are* men's creatures. Now give me your message. Because you *have* a message, I take it? said Ibn Ezra contemptuously: What must I do? Leave for the South? Move my room? Have I spoken out of turn to the gardeners?

—Father, Ramon is eating with us tonight. That is all.
—I see. And I'm to keep out of the way.
—Only since his ideas offend you.

69

—You are not direct, said Ibn Ezra : I see you still have to learn how to deal with me. Tell me what you want.

—We don't keep you here against your will, do we? said the gentle voice sadly.

—Luis no doubt would like me to go, I suppose?

—No. No. It is you who often say it would be better, cried the tormented girl :

—Unfortunately I am too old to travel, said Ibn Ezra : I shall leave when I am fit enough, and not before. As for your husband.

—Please. No curses. No *more* curses.

—The saddest thing is he doesn't even like you does he?

—Father!

—Because you have no self respect.

Miriam tried to stand up, muzzily; determined to open the door and show herself, and bring this unwelcome espionage to an end. But the voices moved off, even as her struggle failed. She heard, from the corner, a quiet breathing. Relief drowned her other thoughts, and she sank back. Clearly, the child at least was recovering. He was the only fixed element in a dissolving world.

When she woke again, it was night. It was as if she had been drugged, the time had run by so fast. And she saw the shutters of her bedroom window were open. Rising, moving towards them, she looked out, for the first time, not on an inner courtyard, the whole house turned inward; but on the streets of Toledo. House after house, with their semi-cylindrical tiles, roofs running together, rose one behind another. She could see that there was a bridge, where two houses actually met, and fused into one. All the streets were dark and winding, with sharp corners; their stones stepped, shallowly, so that donkeys could mount them.

Suddenly, she looked again under the bridgeway, where a gangway joined the two sides of the *callejon,* as if some secret room straddled the street. A woman was letting herself quietly out of the upper part of the house. As Miriam watched, the figure hesitated, and then plunged up into the darkness of a small tunnelway, an even narrower alley, where not even a single donkey could have gone. And then was lost from sight.

Miriam knew it could only be Luis' wife.

5

—Isn't that the bank statement? asked Harriet : There,
underneath *The Times*?

—Oh, the bank statement, said Bernard : Yes. It must
be.

—Aren't you going to open it?

Bernard looked up into his wife's straightforward grey
eyes. She was the very pattern of healthy womanhood, he
thought; full-breasted, wide-hipped, made for the bearing
of children. And he was grateful to her; for the way his
daughters grew gently under her deft hands, and for her
clear grasp on the realities of the world that made it
navigable for them all. But he didn't want to open the
bank statement; and he didn't want the sensible, gloomy
conversation that would follow. He knew he was lucky;
most of his colleagues had wives who took no pleasure in
their role, and spent all their energy on escaping. Harriet
genuinely enjoyed organizing their lives; the details of
ordinary daily existence gave her pleasure. All this he
valued; he wanted it; but all the same his heart beat
uncomfortably fast at the thought of her methodical eye
running over the cheques.

He pretended to be deep in a leading article about
comprehensive education; and after a moment she opened
one of her own letters. It often astonished him that she
found time to keep in touch with so many friends, even
while she baked her own bread, made clothes for the
children, entertained his friends.

—Good heavens, she said now suddenly : Miriam
Garner. She's back in Cambridge.

—Oh?

—She's weirder than ever, of course. Evidently she dined in College last week dressed in layers of Arab jewellery and not much else. They say even Stavros has packed her in, finally. Poor Miriam.

—I don't know about *poor*, said Bernard grumpily : She's a full Professor with tenure, no children, and a few books behind her.

—But she must be so *lonely*. Imagine not having children.

—I thought you were all for the liberation of women?

—Yes, proper nursery schools, equality of opportunity, that sort of thing. But it's just biological to want children, isn't it ? She must be so miserable.

—Oh I don't know. I mean, Bernard added hastily as Harriet's eyebrows rose : People are different aren't they ? They want different things.

—So you think she's perfectly happy ? asked Harriet.

Bernard thought he detected a shade of disappointment in her voice.

—Your description doesn't make her sound particularly subdued, he replied carefully.

—Oh no, I'm sure, she rattled on interminably : But she *is* sick, isn't she ? Do you think perhaps she's frigid ?

—No, said Bernard shortly, standing up.

—You haven't any classes this morning, have you?

—There's a meeting, he said.

—What's the matter?

Bernard's face contorted slightly and he belched.

—Indigestion, he said : Sorry.

Harriet went on reading avidly to herself, while he poured himself another cup of coffee.

—Listen to this, she said.

Enforcedly, he raised his head.

—Last week she had some kind of collapse, read Harriet : They say she's been carted off to Fulbourne.

—Show me that.

73

—Well, hospital anyway, I should think it's Fulbourne.

Bernard's eye raced over the full round handwriting of Harriet's old school friend, and found more information.

—Epilepsy, he murmured : How unpleasant. Well, there are drugs these days, I suppose.

—It says Epilepsy or *some other disorder,* said Harriet darkly. Bernard shut his eyes : Darling, why do you seem to *need* to think of Miriam as mad?

—Now that is a horrid thing to say, Bernard.

—Nevertheless?

—How can I reply, when it's so unfair? I can't *imagine* what you mean.

—All right. Well, said Bernard cheerfully : Luckily I have to be in Cambridge this weekend. So we'll find out.

He had been wondering how to mention a Conference weekend for some days, and now, he knew, it would be very difficult for Harriet to make any protest.

—You are? she said blankly.

—Yes, he said : Isn't that convenient?

Golden Cambridge. Woozy, golden air. Bernard marvelled, tasting it. The air was truly mild and yellow and warm, as farm milk. This bloody city has inherited Autumn, thought Bernard. It is Autumn; October lives in these chestnut leaves. Here the academic year begins with yellow in the birch trees; and *all* the trees keep their leaves dried out in some preternatural sunshine. He remembered this and other things as well as he walked into town from the lock on Chesterton Road, looking at the dark-green, shallow river with boots and bottles resting in the silt at the bottom. Yes, he remembered. Even as he walked. The ducks rippling over the town that lay in the water with the tench. Trees, cyclists, white-painted cottages, deep Prunella, Victorian bay-windows, all caught one metre down under those ducks with iridescent feathers. The sounds rose in the sunshine, as the freshmen called across to one another with their newly found, triumphant voices; as if, just as the city had inherited Autumn, they had personally inherited the city.

And so they had. Arrogant sods, thought Bernard, walking up Portugal Place; looking at assurance already forming on young faces; remembering how he had felt, at eighteen, coming to this peculiar city, to this piece of England that seemed to have gathered all available light into itself, and to be blessed as Bradford was not blessed, nor Hull. As if the Church had chosen its insanitary, fenland site more wisely than it could guess; and could even now lend the glow of exaltation (or was it privilege simply?) to those it once allowed to enter.

Anyway, Bernard thought glumly, it hadn't worked for him, had it? He'd been most unhappy. He'd never really learnt the rules; he was too like his own family up North. However much his gentle, faun-featured friends rebuked and teased him, for battering at them (what an enthusiast he must have been once) with the books he'd found.

—Don't you think? he'd asked, his voice still bewildered as a sixth-former: God damn you, isn't it *true*!

—True? But that's not *really* what we're talking about, is it? Whole thing is more a question of manners, really. And last *weekend*. We were talking about last weekend at Tony's.

Bernard had now reached Magdalene Bridge, and turned towards the triangular cheese-slab of three streets that had once been the heart of Cambridge. Some things had obviously changed. He had to think hard to remember what had once stood where; wondering at whole super-markets thrown-up in the gaps. Heffer's new bookshop,

75

he worked out, must have replaced the cavernous splendours of Matthews, the old-fashioned grocer. There were other new shops; but the street's upper storeys still bulged over the pavement reassuringly and he took a certain pleasure in the way every building had preserved its wood and grouting textures. No doubt it was all for the tourist trade; but he was glad of it.

Bernard looked gloomily into the window of an expensive gentleman's outfitters, and took in the price-tags with incredulity. What about all this new class *mix*, he'd been told about? What young men could possibly afford such clothes, notions of class aside, in England as it was this year? Staring in the window, Bernard gradually became aware that the glass gave him back, on its surface, an image of his own worried, fretful self; dressed, he now saw, in an ill-shapen jacket, which bulged at the buttons. He was used to this. What he minded was not so much the change in his shape, as the sight of his blank, round face. Where had his *eyes* sunken to? God damn it, where was his *soul*? It didn't show any more. Perhaps it was dead? In that case, he thought wretchedly, he might as well have been an *accountant* like his Bradford cousin (who had once said he didn't understand how a Professor could possibly manage on the salary quoted in *The Times*, and to whom Bernard had never dared to explain he was only a Senior Lecturer). But it was false. *False*. I still have an inside, Bernard shrieked silently at the round, bland, face which showed nothing of this turmoil. Don't I feel sad? Read lyric poetry? Love music? My young sensitive spirit can't have gone altogether. Can it?

In desperation, he tried to focus his attention instead on the posters pinned on the green baize between the College crests. And was instantly jolted into a totally different attention by a pink-and-purple notice which advertised :

76

Professor Alexander Stavros:
'Time Travel: The physics of the paranormal'

He read the notice several times thoughtfully. Then he began to walk, in some agitation back towards the Market Square. Paranormal? Paranormal *what*? What the hell was happening to Science, or Physics, or whatever Stavros represented? Was this some obscure fenland madness? He didn't, now he came to think of it, find it difficult to believe in some form of insanity setting in after a few years of perpetual drowsy autumn here. But not in transatlantic Stavros, most brilliant mind of his year; a boy who had actually been interviewed by *The Times* in his second *term* because of a brusque note written to correct an article in *Nature*; the man who had the offer of three Chairs before he was thirty. Paranormal physics of what?

Bemused, he was standing in the market square, smelling apples, and mushrooms, and leaves in the gutter, looking across at David's second-hand book stall, when he noticed that Stavros himself was actually and unmistakably standing there, casually turning over the 10p bargains. His unchanged elegant thin blackness was so unmistakable, that Bernard crossed to greet him without thinking twice. And was rather discomforted to be unrecognized.

—Bernard Hill. You know – Lavatory Court, he was reduced to muttering: We shared the same staircase. Once.

—Yes. My first year here, said Stavros blandly: I remember the misfortune. Of Lavatory court, I mean. Well. It does seem a very long time ago, doesn't it?

He surveyed Bernard from his extra four inches with severe relish; as if detecting every dingy detail of his life. He himself looked exactly as he had a decade earlier; except that he was if anything, paler. It was not,

Bernard felt, going to be easy to question him about the lecture. Paranormal?

—What are you working on? asked Stavros easily: Something French and seventeenth century, I suppose? Not Pascal, is it, you could answer a few questions of mine?

—Probably not, unless they're linguistic, said Bernard, rather unhappily.

Stavros had neatly put his embarrassing finger on an undoubted lacuna in Bernard's command of the period. Not that he couldn't chatter on about Port Royal, of course, but Pascal's physics were another matter. For a moment Bernard suspected Stavros was deceiving him, and remembered exactly who he was.

—Coming to my lecture? asked Stavros with malicious jocularity.

—If I have time, said Bernard, rather hastily.

—Don't put yourself out, said Stavros: It's all in Garner's book, you know. The undergraduates love it.

Then he turned away, and Bernard found he could say no more.

What had Garner been talking about that time on T.V.? Bernard racked his brain, trying to remember, but without much hope of salvaging the occasion. What happened when he watched programmes carefully selected by Harriet with red oblongs in the *Radio Times* as *worthwhile,* was something of which he had long ceased to be ashamed. He sat obediently turned towards the source of information and half-lowered his eyelids. In this way, he had missed painlessly the whole of Kenneth Clark and Bronowski; and almost every Book Programme with an academic on it. Now he came to think of it, Garner had been on a Book Programme; presumably advertising his own book. But for some reason, he had been put alongside a visiting New Yorker, who claimed to be able to draw the strains of music straight from everyone's own brain; and a South American dancer, with an interest in strobe lights, control tape and synthesizers. For some reason Bernard had been struck by the unknown concepts of 'lamination tape', and 'lamination score'; probably because the dancer had been so extraordinarily beautiful. Of Garner's book, unfortunately, he could remember nothing at all.

He wondered if his credit account at Bowes & Bowes was still open. Even if Garner's book turned out to be in paperback, it was probably illustrated with so many mosaics, astrolabes and broken sherds, that Bernard wouldn't otherwise be able to afford it. On the other hand, surely Cambridge could not be so *wholly* dominated by undergraduates richer than their teachers?

The problem solved itself. There, standing next to a boxed-in crate of Penguin copies of Carlos Castañeda, was a pile of books by Octavius Garner under another imprint bearing the same title as Stavros' lecture. Bernard didn't bother to buy one. Clearly, Stavros' intentions were of immaculate respectability. He was sorry for Garner; it was never pleasant to be exposed. But at least, he thought, with the comfort of the warm blue air filling his lungs again as he walked towards his first seminar, at least he didn't need to re-think his whole view of how things stood in the world.

Nothing more logical than to approach the Sidgewick site by means of Garret Hostel Lane, and the magical piece of water between the Wren library and King's. Nevertheless Bernard had only to allow himself to stand still there for a moment and he was lost. A boatload of young people went by, under the falling yellow of the willows and he experienced a strange pang of remorse.

He had taken Harriet along this riverway, fifteen years ago with roses for her birthday; and she had brought Champagne, unbelievably real French Champagne. On just such a golden day. He couldn't remember now how he had even come to be climbing into her boat with his offering; it was casual, he was sure of that. And yet in some way, the Champagne had undone him. Could it have been pure naïveté? Had he thought her *rich*, because her hair was so well-groomed then (Miriam's was wild as a witch); and because she wore stockings. Perhaps it was the stockings? He could still remember the pleasure of putting a hand under her skirt and finding flesh, instead of some chaste web of nylon. Miriam, of course, would have taken her tights off and thrown them in the water if she had wanted to be touched. But she never left you in any uncertainty. Harriet seemed genuinely surprised by his hand, genuinely drunk on two paper cups of Champagne. Oh yes, and genuinely rich, he admitted grimly. She seemed to fit so easily into all those parties where he had felt nervous. Miriam, of course had avoided all that by saying: Good *Christ*, Bernard. What grey friends you have! They make me want to dance on a table and sing rude French songs.

—Please, please, don't though. Will you? He'd begged her.

Whereas the others accepted *Harriet* at once. Yes, they even seemed to find his own Northern presence more tolerable in her tow.

—Bernard? Bernard Hill?

Incredulously Bernard raised his eyes into the present, and saw one of those very young men of his memory standing before him barely changed. He looked as clean as if he had stepped out of cold water; his hair was so freshly washed that small tufts at his temples gleamed.

He was as much a part of the golden landscape as the shining ducks, and the leaves in the grass, and the hanging trees. And in a sense, being a Fellow of Bernard's old college, he had become so.

—I say. What are you up to now?

—Walking about.

—I mean, what have you been doing?

Bernard sighed : Not much.

—You married, I believe.

—Yes.

The youthful face before him smiled in bachelor complacence. This town, Bernard suddenly knew, and the whole scholarly life here, really only worked for bachelors. There was no point in marrying, and bearing children. It was print that had to be borne, and transmitted. Nothing else needed. Monastic Cambridge. True heir to its founding. Except, he supposed hazily, in Science.

—Read Garner's book? said his old college friend.

—No. I saw it in the shops, said Bernard uncertainly : What's it like?

—Apocalyptic clap-trap, laughed the other, as if the note of patronizing dismissal in his voice ought to have been enough. For some reason the confident laugh annoyed Bernard.

—It seems to be selling, though, he said mildly : Doesn't it? What have you been working on?

—Well, of course, muttered his friend; I *am* a full lecturer, now, you know. And Director of Studies. In the Long Vacation, or my next Sabbatical, I *do* hope to get on with several projects. You'll understand.

—Absolutely, said Bernard, rather cheered by the change in tone : Well, I must be off to a seminar now. Good to see you.

And almost uniquely in his experience, he managed to move away from an encounter with his past without regret.

Later that afternoon, he caught a bus from Drummer Street towards Garner's house. He felt no serious apprehensions. No doubt Garner had gone mad. But then, as a supervisor, Garner had always treated Bernard as rudely as if his present state of paranoid delusion had been in full flight for the last twenty years. Perhaps it had. Bernard would not have made the journey out to him at all if either Addenbrooke's or, indeed, Fulbourne, had the slightest record of a Dr Miriam Garner admitted or kept in their wards. Even a diffident telephone call to a private nursing home had produced no information. Unless, therefore, Harriet's letter was a total fraud, he had no choice but to seek out the only person who could presumably help him. If, of course, he would consider doing so, which Bernard rather doubted, as he stood on the broken steps, ringing the bell gloomily, his feet buried over their leather in wet Virginia creeper leaves.

He was taken slightly aback by the girl who opened the door; a skinny, long-haired blonde, who reminded him elusively of Miriam, perhaps only because of the wrapover silk dress she wore. Her face was without expression.

—Yeh? she said : Who are you?

—Well, said Bernard confused : Well. I'm looking for a friend of mine. Miriam Garner. Does her father still live here? He used to be a Professor in the Oriental Languages Department, but he taught me several years back when I was doing an Ancient History paper.

The girl licked her lips as his voice trailed off, and put her head to one side suggestively.

—Have I got the right house? He asked, since she showed no signs of replying.

Looking around he was struck by a profusion of small

ceramics standing on a copper table, engraved with complex antelope and camel designs. He found the ceramics surprising, not only because of their value, but because it was hard to see how anyone could possibly *need* so many jugs at the ready in his hallway.

—It looks as if the Professor's turned to the antique trade, he continued with asperity.

—They're exhibits, she said : You know. For the lecture.

She ran a hand through her hair. Bernard thought it was very remarkable hair; and wondered why there was something a little unattractive about the gesture. It was faintly cautious; almost as if she were wearing a wig. He wondered if she was.

—We got a lot of new stuff, she said, turning herself on to one hip : You should come and hear.

—I'm a historian, he said uncertainly.

—Well that's the point, isn't it?

He recollected his purpose.

—Well. The point is, I'm a friend of Professor Garner's *daughter.*

—Oh Yes. Are you? Close?

—I believe she's been ill, said Bernard : I'd like to get in touch with her.

—Do you want to leave a note? asked Cressida.

—Look, said Bernard : someone here must know where she is. Surely? Can I speak to Professor Garner please? *He'll* remember me, I think, said Bernard with diminishing certainty in his voice.

—I don't know if he'll come down. He can be a real sod, said the girl casually.

She paused at the bottom of the stairs.

—Not a biochemist, are you?

—No. I told you.

—Good. We've had some trouble with an American biochemist. I mean I can *tell* you aren't American. Are you a Jew?

83

Bernard stated : No.

The question made him uneasy. He'd always heard Garner was.

—He's had some funny letters.

A loud, gruff voice made itself heard from the top of the stairs.

—Cressida. Shut that door, will you?

Bernard shifted his weight nervously; not sure if the instruction was to push him *out* or hold him *in*. As the old man approached, he realized the answer was, quite simply, neither. Garner had not noticed him.

—Find my glasses Cressy, there's a darling, said Garner in an unfamiliar wheedling voice.

Bernard coughed : Professor Garner, I'm sorry to disturb you; to break in on you, I hope you remember me? My name is Hill. I'm a friend of your daughter. Could you tell me how I can get in touch with her?

—Cressida, said Garner : my glasses. They're somewhere in the bedroom.

He tilted back his head, meanwhile, and tried to focus black suspicious eyes on Bernard.

—My daughter? Now what makes you ask that? She's never taken any interest in me, never comes to see me you know. Hasn't for years.

—Professor Garner, Miriam was in Cambridge. This week.

—There you are then. Shows you. Didn't even bother to look me up.

—I hear she's ill, said Bernard : Aren't you interested?

—How do *you* know she's ill? said the old man craftily.

—Glasses, said Cressida.

Garner put them on and stared at Bernard reflectively : You're a journalist, aren't you?

Bernard was furious.

—Sir, my name is Dr Hill. I *used* to be your pupil. No doubt ten years have aged me out of all recognition, but no-one has ever told me that I look like a *journalist*. I wish, said Bernard : I did. Or could afford to. I'm a historian. I was at University here the same year as your daughter. We did Ph.D.s together.

—From the *Jewish Chronicle* I shouldn't wonder, muttered Octavius, as if nothing had been said. He sat down abruptly : And the silly thing is, I *could* help them. If they weren't so paranoid. No-one wants to listen.

—Look here, began Bernard : My wife had a letter telling us the whole story. There's no point going on like this.

—What? What story?

—Of Miriam's illness, said Bernard, hopelessly : I don't know why you're so secretive. There's no need to be ashamed about epilepsy these days.

He looked in appeal at Cressida, again struck by the familiarity of the printed silk. He could also detect a marked erotic interest in her attentive gaze, which for some reason was fixed on his belly.

Professor Garner patted his own forehead, with a green silk handkerchief.

—Do you know where Miriam is now? said Bernard directly. The question affected Garner badly. He put his head back on the stairs and moaned.

—That's just the blood going out of his head, said Cressida : Don't look so anxious; he often does that.

—It *looks* very nasty.

—Brandy, murmured the ashen lips.

Cressida said : Naughty man, you know what brandy does to you? We'll go and get you some water. Come on, she nodded to Bernard.

He followed nervelessly; feeling fairly guiltless at leaving the sick man, because he had himself observed the sharpness in Garner's eyes masked by the fallen lids. Also, since the girl clearly fancied him, she seemed likely to let out information, he told himself. If only by accident.

85

The kitchen smelled strongly of fresh paint; the walls were bare and white. Cressida went on into the scullery; and Bernard waited thoughtfully as he heard her running a tap. It was then he noticed the tin of peaches. Standing on the table, the tin was unremarkable at first; except that it had been opened badly. The metal was all jagged, as though someone had made a desperate attempt to prise the lid off with a tent skewer. What was extraordinary, however, was the single peach at the bottom. It was the peach that drew Bernard's attention. Because it was blue. Fringes of blue mould were growing out of its soft flesh. Bernard wondered: how long in normal conditions did it take a mould to grow in sugar solution? Sugar, the ancient preservative.

—What you looking at? said Cressida.

Bernard gestured: That disgusting object. It's a wonder you haven't gone down with Salmonella.

—Doesn't grow in vegetables. Does it?

—What's the peach doing there?

Cressida hesitated. Then she put the glass of water on the table and walked towards him, eyes shut, lips apart; straddling her body before him.

—You don't want to *worry* so much, she breathed.

Bernard felt prickles of panic in his neck muscles. Cressida stepped out of her shoes.

—Well, but I wanted to ask, he said, backing to the wall.

The childlike face approached his own, mouth open; rather like a voracious flower-animal. With a quick nervous gesture, he took the back of her golden-haired skull, and pressed her face into his shoulder. Cressida sighed, misunderstanding him, and pressing her small body closely into his own.

—About Miriam, he said huskily.

With his hand he explored her neck, at the nape, feeling for the tell-tale signs of false hair.

—I said, she'll be all right, said Cressida, moving her prominent and bony mound of Venus into his crotch.

Bernard's heart gave a series of unwelcome leaps.

—Cressida. Where the bloody hell's my drink of water? came a powerful yell from the hallway.

—Don't you think we ought to help him, Bernard pleaded.

—Listen. He's *fine* now, isn't he? said Cressida, with her eyes still shut.

Bernard put two hands on her shoulders: Later, he promised equivocally.

She sighed: You're really so beautifully *fat,* she marvelled.

—Well. Thank you. However – what can we do about it *now?* Bernard reasoned, as he might with a cannibal.

—Cressida!

—I love fat men. Don't go, wait here.

She moved away from him slowly. With mute horror, he saw the long blonde hair was askew. He did not mention it.

—Later, she repeated.

Then she picked up the glass of water, and moved away, her tongue still flicking between her lips; as she turned to meet his eyes a convulsion shook her visibly.

It wasn't easy to get upstairs. For at least ten minutes Bernard stood with eyes shut leaning against the wall and listening to the Professor's groans and protestations mixed with occasional grunts of effort from Cressida. Even when he heard them both moving firmly across the hallway into the library, he hesitated before moving. Could he be seen through an open door? Feeling like an adulterer, he took off his shoes, and began to creep out of the kitchen towards the staircase. To his relief the doors of both rooms were shut.

87

He ran up the broad stairs in his socks, reached the landing and then stopped, baffled. There were several rooms to try. And he was afraid. Partly of the lustful Cressida, no doubt; but partly for no reason at all. As he hesitated, the door of the far room opened and closed briskly. Bernard gaped. It was Stavros.

—Well if it isn't little Bernie, said Stavros, not unkindly, but clearly as surprised as Bernard himself.

—What are *you* doing here?

—Sick visiting, said Stavros.

—Who's in that room? said Bernard thickly.

I'm really quite *heavy*, he consoled himself. Stavros' *arms* are long, but I suppose I could always butt him with my head.

Stavros approached him thoughtfully. He didn't seem aggressive, or criminally inclined.

—It's Garner's daughter, I thought you knew, he said quietly: It's all a frightful scandal, really.

—Can I see her?

Stavros paused: Yes. She won't know you, I'm afraid. You'd better be prepared, it's not pleasant. Of course Garner's got a full-time nurse, and the instruments alone would have M.I.T. costing very carefully. She's on full life-support, you see. You'd better be prepared for that. Artificial respirator, heart control, everything.

—She can't talk?

—She's like a very lovely vegetable.

—Then how do you know? In what sense is she alive?

—Well, said Stavros: There are very strong eye movements. They correlate with brain patterns.

—I don't understand you, yelled Bernard.

—Quietly. Do you want Garner up here?

—Sorry. Say that again, would you?

—She's *dreaming*, said Stavros.

Bernard thought about that: How horrible.

—Wait a while. Before going in to see her.

—Well.

—Tell me, said Stavros conversationally: Do you think Garner is mad?

Bernard stared: Clinically? I've no idea.

—Well, he's not. He's written a perfectly sensible book. It's not his fault the nutters have picked it up for the wrong reasons. People don't want peace, said Stavros: They want bombs. Look at the papers. People love bombs. Bombs, air disasters and political tyranny. And do you know why? The whole attraction of reading about the End of it All is their own rotten little lives don't matter any more. That's *why* they did all those mad calculations about the Apocalypse in the seventeenth century, right? Took their mind off plagues and all the marauding soldiers, going about raping and killing. John wrote *his* gospel with one eye on the miserable buggers; they always love it. People just can't *bear* to be singled out to die, can they? They'd rather the whole world went with them. Haven't you noticed? That's why they get so excited by Black Holes.

When the sky is split and the stars are scattered
when the seas are loosed and the graves are exposed

—That's not John, said Bernard quickly.

—No, it's the Koran. Well, I mean it's everywhere, I just like that bit. Have you ever lived in America?

—Only in Boston.

—Yes. Well, you could be quite surprised further over. I like Islamic food you know, said Stavros, with no sign of moving into the irrelevant: Fat and salt and peppers; all the peppers: bay and savoury; sesame seeds; have you ever eaten pigeon and quail cooked with theriac?

—Miriam, said Bernard miserably: What's happened? What can be done? There must be something to be done.

—Must there? I think you'd better come and see, said Stavros.

89

6

—Gone? said Ibn Ezra: How very interesting.

Now that Miriam saw him squat and thick on his cushion, next to Luis, it was unmistakable why the power in the household lay with him. He was an ugly man; but there was a sharp intelligence in his ugliness. It tightened his lips, and narrowed his eyes. Luis's lips were slack and wet, and the lower lip fell open; so that although his physical presence suggested considerable strength, under Ibn Ezra's eye he looked tamed, domesticated. And stupid. His clothes were far more ornate than Ibn Ezra's; but although as owner of so magnificent a house they ought to have seemed appropriate, they had a kind of brashness in them. A declaration of spendthrift decadence, and laziness. Moreover, his eyes on Miriam were covert and pink with lechery.

—Nine children, said Ibn Ezra sadly: And a good wife bore them all.

Luis shifted his weight, but did not otherwise indicate impatience. Miriam decided there must be some other sanction Ibn Ezra wielded, since Luis did not have the marks of one who respected intelligence.

—My sons, said Ibn Ezra: At least my sons inherited my sense. I call it sense, not wit. Though they had that also. They knew how to take vineyards and make them prosper; and still they respected a man who wanted to leave his mark on more than the land. Before he goes into it. They were farmers; and they were scholars. Unfortunately, both married rashly. One lost his nose for his mistake, and the other is somewhere in the North of Europe, passing for a Christian. I love them both, said Ibn Ezra, with a glance of ill-concealed contempt at his son-in-law : When I die my money shall be theirs if they can be found.

Luis' face became a trace more sullen.

—Otherwise, God was pleased to send me daughters. Seven daughters. Some died but most of them were beautiful.

—Were they also disobedient ? enquired Miriam.

—No. No, said Ibn Ezra : Soft as butter. They married easily, they gave birth within a year. But one after another they died; and their children were all girls. I do not blame their husbands for marrying again.

—And to all of them you gave great dowries, burst out Luis : Only not to my wife.

—Esther, poor Esther, said Ibn Ezra : Still, you didn't need my money, Luis. Did you ?

He mused awhile.

—It is a waste of money to give gold to fools.

—Meaning ? said Luis hotly.

Ibn Ezra laughed : She was so sad, my poor Esther. So old, and not beautiful. Why should she be married for her dowry ? We played *Shakhmat* and were both mistaken. Weren't we ? Stale mate. A bad game. Still I don't hate you as I did. She is loyal, and serves you well, I expect. I wonder where she has gone ?

Miriam repressed an exclamation of muted anger.

As it happened she knew exactly where Esther was; although she had obediently told her story of the evening flight, as commanded. Not only did she know where the girl was, she had hidden her in her own room, and was still recovering from the accidental encounter. Because Esther, though she might seem ugly to these sensual fools

91

obsessed with tits and thighs, had a face more beautiful than Miriam had ever seen; a familiar face, also; though the familiarity was not so easy to pin down. Nor did she strike Miriam as old. She was unquestionably small; but her arms and wrists were delicately covered with flesh; perhaps her proportions were therefore unexpected; but she was not boyish, although her breasts were small, and she had as little fat on her hips as a young boy. Perhaps her face was a little thinner and longer than oval; but the features were perfectly pure and even; the nose straight and small, with almost invisible nostrils, the lips slender and yet filled with flesh, and her teeth were white and even as the white seeds in the mouth of her child. And Esther's smile was of such a peculiar tenderness, that Miriam's heart ached to hear her shortcomings discussed so callously.

—Hide me, Esther had said : I am terrified.

—Some women, said Luis : are a mistake of God. Such a one you gave me for a wife.

—Still she is learned, said Ibn Ezra, with a yellow-fanged grin of agreement : Give her the job of managing your accounts ! When she was at home with me, I found her excellent at such matters. You do not make *use* of her abilities, Luis.

Miriam shivered.

—I can hire a clerk cheaply enough.

—What is the matter? Luis asked Miriam.

—I think I have some kind of fever.

—Fevers are not to be neglected.

—Then let me go and lie down.

—Don't wander off, said Ibn Ezra.

—I shall be in the room you gave me. Don't worry, said Miriam : I have nowhere to go.

—Luis, leave us, said Ibn Ezra.

—Men! said Miriam, with a grimace, misinterpreting the instruction.

—Why should *you* frown on men? asked Ibn Ezra: You are not ill-favoured. And not all men are like that fool Luis. Listen. I want to make you my daughter. I like you. You speak up fluently without being shrill. That is unusual. Also I notice you avoid weeping, which is always a relief. Will you allow me to find you a husband? And give you a dowry?

—I don't understand. This is all wrong. Why should you so slight your own daughter? cried Miriam despairingly: Or her son?

—She is not to my liking, muttered Ibn Ezra.

—Well, then supposing you stop liking me? Couldn't that happen? Supposing my husband stops loving me? Who shall I go to for help?

—Anywhere you wish, except the Church.

—There would be nowhere to go, said Miriam, with a peculiar sinking in her own belly: Would there? But why the Church? Have you some reason to fear Christians?

—The *Church,* not Christians! I work with Christians. I can read Latin, and write in the Romance languages. They have come even from the North, from a far cold country to read with my help; to learn Arithmetic, Algebra and Astrology from me. All of them were good men; and still they had a strange poison in them. They did not trust me. They had been taught in their most sacred book not to trust me.

—And the Moslems?

—Well, the Malikites. *They* were ignorant of what they did when they burnt the books of al-Ghazal. I hear bad stories of their treatment of scholars. Yes. Jews and Christians have been forced to empty rubbish and clean latrines. There is always danger. But the Fall, daughter, the Fall will not come through them. It will come as a

Crusade, over the Pyrenees, and it will be led by holy men of the Church. The stars declare it, concluded Ibn Ezra.

—All that is as may be, said Miriam: Meanwhile my head is reeling with pain. Can't you see I'm a sick woman?

—Truly? said Ibn Ezra, without moving: Sick women do not rise and pace about. What is disturbing you?

—I was wondering why you had sent Luis away.

—And where he has gone perhaps?

—Perhaps. Ibn Ezra, said Miriam urgently: Help your daughter! It is not your daughter who sent for the priest, I am sure of it. And Luis means some harm to the child. Don't you care? He is your grandson, after all.

—I see that you *are* delirious, said Ibn Ezra coldly: What you say is complete fantasy. Go to your room. You disappoint me.

—Thank you. I'm going, said Miriam.

But at the door she could not resist adding: I see your favour is lost quite rapidly, Ibn Ezra.

—Hold me, he says in the night: Hold me. Surround me. And I obey him. And still he shakes with fear. Every night he explains how he cannot sleep. He likes to sleep in the day, he feels safe.

Miriam remembered the terror. Walked towards it. This time she would press her questioning, she determined.

—How did you come to marry such a buffoon? she asked Esther.

—Well, at first he was *kind*. He is a kind man, you know. It was time for him to marry; and for me it was almost too late. Of course I accepted, if only to be a married woman; to be no longer a slave to my father who always disliked me.

—*Why* did he dislike you?

—How do I know? My narrow hips make few children.

—It isn't the hips, it's the pelvis. In childbearing.

—Is it? Well then because I don't look healthy. Miriam said: Your eyes are so lovely. *Not* Asiatic. Deep.

—But they are dim. So I look scared, like a frightened rat. People laugh when I stumble. They took my child from me, because I once fell holding him.

—Can you see me?

—Only your shape. Your solid face. Yes. But not your expression. I couldn't read my father's either. For years I tried to guess what my father's expression was. And then one day I came up close and kissed him, and I saw: It was *disgust*.

—You're wrong. He says you are more intelligent than other women.

—Harder working. More anxious to please. Perhaps because he despises all those things in women. Even my sister, whom I do not mean to speak of; he preferred *her* spirit.

—Does he? One of your dead sisters, you mean?

—No, No. The *other*. She ought not to be spoken of, because my father has forbidden her name to be mentioned. And yet, do you know, even she (poor girl – I do not know if she lives any longer in Toledo) even *she* has been endowed with a part of my father's goods? I, and I alone he hates. I don't know why.

—It must be your goodness.

—Why do you say I am good?

—Because goodness is in your face, said Miriam: Just as anyone can see the spendthrift lout in Luis' mouth.

—Nevertheless, said Esther sadly: I could have loved Luis. If it were not for the nights. He tells me about his whores. How they are made. They have muscles in their

95

bellies, where I feel nothing. When they want to, they can clasp a man inside them as if with hands. And so they learn to give men pleasure. Do you believe that?

Miriam said, reluctantly: Women who make love do find that *happens*. But I'm not sure how voluntary it is. At least I never found it so. I suppose, with practice, it could become like any other set of muscles.

—Vile. Isn't it vile? How can they bear the stink, these women? Do you know he and Ramon shared a woman. Last week they went one after another. Into her. She had no time even to *wash* between them.

Miriam began to feel embarrassed. Clearly part of the purity in Esther's face sprang from a singular distaste for sexuality.

—A convent, she said as if to herself: Would be your only sanctuary.

Terror crossed Esther's face.

—Nevertheless, though I have spoken to nuns, I did not call *that* priest, said Esther: He is from Burgundy and it is Luis who has brought him here. I fear him, hate him. He is Ramon's man.

—Send him away, then, said Miriam, surprised.

—But I dare not.

—Why? What can he do? The Church has no jurisdiction in this house.

—Luis called for him. He will be angry. He will do terrible things to me if I disobey him.

—What will he do? There are laws in Toledo, I hear. Let him divorce you, it sounds as if it would be your good fortune.

—My son would suffer.

—Your son is well now, said Miriam: Listen. I will go and discuss the priest for you. Luis will not hurt me. I am sure.

As she spoke, both women looked up at the shaft of light entering the room.

—And what makes you so sure of that? said Luis: It seems Ramon was right to treat you with suspicion. I blame my own weakness for beauty. I have spent some time talking to the priest, and he says categorically your treatment was unknown to him. I am much afraid this bold lady is some kind of witch.

—The child is well, isn't he? cried Esther.

For the first time Miriam saw Ramon in the doorway. He was not slack-faced like his friend; but thin and wiry as the priest had been. He looked at both women as if the idea of their suffering gave him profound pleasure.

—Bring them both, he said.

7

—We are all, said Stavros casually: time-travellers, out of necessity; which is to say, we expect to move in a direction we are pleased to call *forward,* at a speed we have learnt to measure plausibly by the use of clocks and calendars; and we would insist this description of our progress is adequate for normal purposes, which it is. Right? Now my purpose is to up-end that particularly comfortable view of the world tonight, and suggest the possibility of other modes of progression.

He began to pace across the small raised platform thoughtfully, hands clasped at his blue velvet back like an Edwardian. The huge audience waited. The lecture-hall originally booked (which held only a hundred and fifty), had been changed in face of a press of people; upward of five hundred, probably, and Bernard and Harriet had gained, as a result of the mass migration, two good seats in the centre of the fifth row. Harriet promptly took off her coat, muffling-hood and gloves; and got out a notebook and pencil. Bernard found himself looking round to see who, exactly, made up the vast audience; recognizing two eminent faces from the Biological Sciences who had been equipped with microphones; and observing that Oriental Languages and History were well represented. Undergraduates filled every other available stair and niche. It was rather startling, at five o'clock, to be part of such an audience, with the day going out of the windows; and the hall darkening; and beams of light that picked out Stavros' face, with luminous clarity.

Harriet was wearing her glasses, and Bernard saw she had already made a note or two, in her neat hand. Uneasily, he assessed her posture of concentration, and her expression of joyful intensity. At first he could not put a name to it, though he had seen her wear it before, over breakfast, reading *The Guardian*. With reluctance, he identified the lip-licking certainty as righteous indignation. All her gods were under attack, he realized suddenly : commonsense, the rational world, the ordinary decencies. With sudden anxiety he wondered if she was planning to ask a question.

—There are several eminent historians of Science in this assembly, who will not blench to admit the extraordinary flexibility of what we are pleased to call knowledge. All bizarre phenomena are paranormal until they are explained. Perhaps the audience at large should be reminded that electricity and phenomenology were not so long ago taken *equally* seriously (which is to say *mocked* equally) by an eminent F.R.S.; and that within living memory the whole idea of travel into *space* outside the atmosphere of the earth was dismissed as poppycock by a great scientist, who is still alive, known to you all (and will of course be named by me if anyone *really* wants to challenge me privately). Science is not always in need of correction of course, any more than the medieval Church was always wrong. But it does have a body of *dogma* to defend, rather in the same way. It has almost as many servants doing so; though the power to silence dissent in the west is more or less financial in scope, nevertheless its power of ridicule is extremely potent in this cause.

Bernard's attention wandered. The undergraduates were enjoying the attack on Science, he saw : altogether Science was in retreat at the moment, badly confused

99

with technology which everybody hated. It was, Bernard
thought, *odd*, remembering the glamour that had
attached to Science in his own day; the defensiveness of
the Arts faculties; their prim claims to be the guardians
of moral values; the sheer confident assertiveness of
scientific progress.

—In dreams begin responsibilities, said Stavros, with a
little self-mockery.

—Whoever is that peculiar girl waving at us, Bernard?
asked Harriet.
—Where? said Bernard, turning hastily away from a
vision of Cressida in purple satin on the front row, and
looking, for safety, into the audience behind him.
—There, *idiot*! The one with frizzled short hair
next to Garner. Good heavens, she's standing up. Surely
you can see her now?
—Ah yes. I see, said Bernard, waving back and nodding
distantly : Must be some mistake.
—But what an extraordinary way to behave! In the
middle of a lecture.
   Cressida put her arm round Garner, whispered something in his ear, and the old man turned to peer behind
him.
—She certainly treats the Professor very intimately.
Harriet appeared hypnotized : But she's grotesque. That
hair! It's been *permed*. She looks like something from the
twenties. What is she wearing, satin? It's horrible.
—She is alarming, agreed Bernard.
—But she's going up on the platform.
—I think, said Bernard sadly : She must be part of the
act.

And, oh God, Miriam, thought Bernard. The shaft of memory pierced him through layers of tranquillizer. Nothing could block the pain of those red tubes and white tubes. The white block and plastic cover. The monitored heart-rate on a small screen, like a hesitant green version of the telly tennis he'd played in pubs or railway stations. And the white room humming like the hold of a ship. The hum of machines; to breathe, change her blood, feed her, and help her piss. To keep life going. While Stavros said : Funny to think of all Garner's money going into these pieces of machinery. He's had to sell a lot of his finds, you know.

—It is not for me to expound here the historical details of Professor Garner's book, which I am sure most of you will have read in any case; the basic vision of a Europe fallen into division through the triumphant incursion of the Church militant into an area of tolerance and open-minded discovery is not my subject; though *my* allegiance is clear. I shouldn't be surprised to find the Inquisition had its defenders. What I am sure interests you as it did me, was the Professor's claim to have used Arabic and Cabbalistic number magic to gain *physical* entry into that period. Now had the learned Professor claimed to have met a magnificently handsome Spaniard from the plateau-area who said to him : shut your eyes, smoke this, and you will arrive in eleventh century Toledo, I should have had no personal difficulty in deciding my response. But the Professor is a rather abstemious man; he is more excited by documents than drugs; about which he is rather nervous. And the conformations of Arabic patterning, and their relationship to simple mathematical propositions, were interesting enough in themselves for me to explore these principles last year, out of curiosity, and without any particular conviction, with the aid of a West Coast computer. I should not have come before you tonight, if I did not have one or two experiments aside from computer tapes to present. It is an area of maximum scepticism, but there is every hope of testing the essential core of Professor Garner's hypothesis.

—Isn't this *disgraceful*, breathed Harriet into Bernard's ear : What *is* Stavros doing, taking part in this fraud?
—We have here, said Stavros : a number of crystal spoons, from eleventh-century Toledo, which I have asked the present incumbent of the Chair of Archaeology to come forward, and examine, while I continue.
—Good Christ, said Harriet : Surely he isn't going to claim Garner brought them back with him from a trip?

Miriam. Miriam, thought Bernard. With three green-masked girls in attendance, moving quietly about their work, taking note of the changes on the dials; going to drawers where quivers of catheters lay alongside disposable syringes, and long needles. Miriam's body covered by machinery, entered by drips; connected to suction tubes. Bernard could hardly bring himself to look at her face.
—What is that?
—The Bird Ventilator. It's a gas-flow respirator. That's a water hose. Over there is the kidney dialysis system. And the E.C.G. records any change in potassium, any disturbance. Those are blood pressure cuffs.
—She is so pale. And what are they doing to her?
—The nurses have to see that there is no drying up of the cornea. Every day she has to be turned over at

regular intervals. And they have to change the bedding, which is naturally damp with secretions, fistulas, perspiration and occasional diarrhoea.

—Stop it, Stavros. Please. Can't something be done? To help her escape from this?

—Something?

—To cure her.

—At first they talked about *status epilepticus*. That's when the respirator became necessary. But now they really don't know. I'm sorry. You look sick.

—It's horrible. She's not real. She's not *here*, let alone alive, Bernard had said staring at the multiply restrained body.

—Oh, I don't know about that. Does it really matter so much if she is out of touch with the realities of this *room*. This *town*? What about the rest of us, licensed to go about as much inside our own heads for all spiritual purposes as she is? Are *we* here?

—Don't be flippant. We can move can't we? Touch and feel?

—Some people wouldn't care all that much about touching and feeling. As long as they could think, imagine. And dream.

—Who? Who are these *people,* raged Bernard : I don't know them.

—Well, I suppose it depends how well you ever knew Miriam. I find it peculiarly fitting.

—And how did this ever *happen*? demanded Bernard.

Stavros was drawing on the board a series of rather elegant Moorish decorative patterns. The first Bernard recognized as the concentric rings of a Vedic square.

—Obviously, Stavros was saying : This is a number series with a distinctive rhythm, though we cannot represent this in the form of a graph without cabbalistic reduction.

103

Bernard looked about to see who was following. One or two mathematicians were taking notes; but the hall was generally, he felt, expectant. Waiting. All this was a kind of lead-in of respectability to assertions more outrageous.

—The moving point leaves a trace we call a line; and the moving line leaves a trace we call a plane. The imaginary inhabitants of a two dimensional world would see only lines. As long as our internal model is convincing, then we will be undeterred by meeting new experience. But we all, rightly fear chaos. Let us now take a more complex pattern source, a number series which fascinated Leonardo of Pisa who brought it to Europe in 1228 after studying with the Arabs.

On the platform Cressida yawned hugely, her jaws agape to one side, and made no attempt to cover her mouth. When the paroxysm ended her eyes sought Bernard's. With horror, he lip-read her whispered message : Lovely FAT man.

—Is she saying something? asked Harriet, who appeared remarkably alert.

—Shh. I'm trying to follow.

—I hope the simpler vocabulary of pattern in Islamic decoration will be now clear enough, so that we can move on to a visual language capable of unlocking concepts of greater complexity.

Stavros paused, took the pulse of the audience with the experienced lecturer's quick flick and set aside several pages.

—The Islamic vision came from a people who had learnt to navigate deserts, he said smiling, his blue eyes moving about the rows of students, who shuffled under his gaze :

It is not surprising they took careful note of the movement of the stars. Let me show you how the stars as the Arabs saw them became a circular graph of the Vedic square. And let me lead you towards that aesthetic fusion of intellect and intuition which Professor Garner's book explores. This involves a fundamental faith in a dynamic order present in the physiology of the brain. I hope colleagues will support me in saying that recent research into the structure of brain-rhythms suggest that our apprehension of time in particular may need serious revision along his lines.

Perhaps Stavros is mad. But where was she, *Miriam*? Bernard thought. Remembering how he had in a flash before waking that very morning lain across her younger body, pressed himself into her, Miriam, Miriam, waiting in a paradise of certainty, for joy which he reached between an alarm bell and the shake of Harriet's hand? Poor Miriam in her white world, stunned out of every natural function. He looked at the lecture hall clock. Was this really going to continue for another three-quarters of an hour?

—Bernard, hissed Harriet.

Stavros wrote four bold symbols on the board.
—The language of the spirit, it seems, and the language of Mathematics are close. These four symbols serve both as a word and a number, as any Hebrew scholar can tell me. But the early Cabbalists only dreamed of wresting *prophecies* out of words. Innocent men! Our purpose was quite new. We wanted to *speak* to the unconscious mind and receive replies in detail. For that, we needed

something as simple as the computer's binary code. To direct the spirit back through the centuries. And then to monitor what could be seen. *This* system was to be our answer.

While Miriam in her white and polystyrene lung, with those tubes and that catheter in her, presumably wandered in her own dream; unreachably. How lonely it was, dreaming, thought Bernard.

—No lonelier than an artist, Stavros had suggested the day before: Look she is creating her own world. She moves in it like a poet or a musician. You put too big a value on what you call reality.

—It's all there *is,* said Bernard doggedly.

—Bernard, you aren't following.

—Yes I am.

—Then can't you see the logical flaw? It's the most stupendous piece of *léger de main.*

—I'm *trying* to *listen,* goddamn it.

—I don't know how many of you are familiar with the work of the tenth-century Persian experimental philosopher, Ibn Sina. My scientific colleagues will forgive me if I just explain that for him the universe was a cosmos of symbols; which is to say, not of *external* fact, but *interior* reality; put more sharply there could be *no* possible separation for him that would have a meaning. He describes how the first point acted upon by nature forms a line; which in turn forms a plane; and then a body; and there is nothing strange to him in extending this to body-in-movement or what we should call the fourth dimension. This is the point to explain precisely the methods we have used to enter such a dimension in a controlled manner.

Stavros paused impudently.

—Methods, repeated Stavros cheerfully.

Bernard had a sense of a general leaning forward in the audience, as though the lecture had begun to touch for the first time on some desirable area of knowledge. Bernard himself speculated, on the nature of the claim to be made.

—How exactly, Stavros asked : did we *manage* to loosen the ties that normally connect mind and body? Some experiments using ancient rituals have been reported from the University of California recently; Professor Garner *does* mention these in his book. But, aside from the years of training demanded, such methods are always open to suspicion; we have seen altogether too many *gurus* haven't we? What I needed as a scientist was a subject with no conceivable point of view to push; an *innocent* subject. And so we turned to other ways of inducing trance-like conditions. Hypnotic drugs, strobe lighting, and certain forms of sexual excitation all appeared to precipitate states of timelessness spontaneously in one certain class of subject : namely, women with a mild tendency towards epilepsy.

Stavros paused : Now the dangers of such procedure are obvious. At any moment the cord that links us to our ghost-like selves is frail. To put that delicate strand under tension lightly would be unforgivable. Some of the trips Professor Garner reports have been merely glimpses; others have involved a prolonged wandering of the spirit. For these extended trips it has been necessary to monitor all the body's vital functions meticulously. . . .

Bernard sat up suddenly, knocking Harriet's pen to the

floor and rousing little hisses of disapproval all around him. In his agitation, he barely noticed this. Stavros continued to talk and drew diagrams on the board. He talked about correcting the Toledo map of the heavens. He talked about astrology. Everyone listened passionately except Bernard.

—But I am sure you are impatient to meet Professor Garner's prime witness.

At this he nodded towards Cressida, who blinked and shrugged rather sullenly. Then she got up awkwardly, put one hand behind her back and made a formal bow to the audience, rather in the manner of an eighteenth-century footman. She then glared with great hostility at the waiting hall and said loudly: You said they would clap now.

There were a few nervous stutters of applause.

—Could we now have the rock crystal spoons, Professor, asked Stavros gaily: I take it you agree we have dated them correctly? Miss Cressida Garner will now explain how she came to find them.

—Garner? Well, I didn't know Miriam had a sister, but now I come to look –

—Will you bloody shut up, said Bernard.

—Darling there's no need to be rude, is there?

Cressida stood and took hold of the microphone, her whole body clenched with nervousness; her head poked out and forward on her neck in a posture of comic awkwardness, which at the same time gave an impression of hostility and resentment. She stared round the audience for a long time, presumably finding her voice; and the audience stirred restlessly. But when she began to speak her voice had a steady vibrant whine which penetrated very clearly to the back of the hall. The monotone suggested she had learnt what she had to say by heart.

—I don't think you should all be sitting here *looking* at *me* because Professor Garner is a great man, you should all know that anyway. And I only did what he said; it makes me sad I never *could* do what he really wanted. These spoons I just found in the sand, I think maybe people who might have been running away from Toledo left them; only I never got through the walls of the city, you see I was always afraid he would be angry about that. Only, he said we could always try again, and the maths was wrong; so when Professor Stavros came I thought we'd work it out. Only *he* made me frightened I would mess everything up; and he wanted to use his machine, and tried to teach me a message to say. Things like that.

She stopped and peered into the hall : Every *time* Professor Stavros said it would be different; but I always found myself on the wrong side of the Tagus.

There was a ripple of suppressed laughter.

She gave a convulsive shrug : Yeah. So I poked around again and found something. And I got back. It's very *good* to get back, I think; the Professor was always pleased to see me.

A flash-bulb smoked in the hall.

—No pictures. There were to be *no* pictures ! yelled the Chairman : The Professor insisted. Confiscate that camera.

For a moment the Hall erupted in furious noise. Then Cressida continued in the same flat voice.

—Anyway, I can't see why everyone is making such a fuss; about slipping about in time; why shouldn't we?

Harriet said: I wonder if she's on largactil Bernard? You aren't listening; have you gone to sleep?
—No.

Cressida concluded: I mean the fact that I should have to *stand* here! The way you all sit so politely and *wait*! I mean what more do you expect to be *given*? It's just *awful*! You ought just to *understand*, without any of this, it's disgusting.

Then she sat down, to a scatter of applause which was thin, embarrassed, and led by the enormous (amplified) efforts of the Chairman, who hastened to beg Stavros back into a central position.
—Professor Alexander Stavros has kindly agreed to answer questions. In view of the extraordinary nature of this occasion I should be grateful if I could call first on our prize-winning physicist. . . .

Bernard gripped Harriet's arm: There's no need for you to speak.
—Why ever not?
—Please. I mean.
—Well if everyone goes on politely beating around the bush like that, I'll have to.
—Harriet, I swear I'll hit you if you open your mouth.
—Bernard. What on earth has happened to you?

A Scottish voice from the back of the hall asked if Professor Garner could be given a microphone. Stavros cheerfully handed his own across to him, and sat down without apparent anxiety. The Professor peered upward at his interlocutor.

—Professor Garner, as a long-standing admirer of your work to re-establish a sense of the importance of the Moslem world, it bothers me very much to see you, even whimsically, entering the areas you have heard Professor Stavros and – er – Miss Garner describe. Let us take first these spoons, which you report this lady gave you without any knowledge of their worth. You must understand that the *authenticity* of the spoons, or even their dating by experts is absolutely irrelevant. Look. *Here* are two spoons, which I would be grateful if someone would take very gently from me, and hand up to Professor Garner? Have you received them, sir? Do you not agree with me they also look genuine? Well, you are quite right and you are at liberty to test them as far as you wish, because they *are* genuine. But they come from my own museum in Edinburgh, and they should be. Which museum do yours come from, I wonder? He sat down amid a certain stir, just this side of applause, as the audience took the point he was making. Professor Garner said nothing. Stavros moved quickly across to take back the microphone.
—Thank you. It would of course be a simple matter for anyone to deceive the public at large in the way you suggest. However, no doubt you'd agree the spoons are rare?
—Yes. So please be careful with them.
  The uneasy audience rippled with muted laughter.
—In that case, they are no doubt insured?
—Of course, said the Scottish voice, impatiently.
—Precisely. And the number of spoons of this kind you must realize are in no way a secret from insurance companies. I have here, ladies and gentlemen, a general statement from Lloyds, which would be too long to read here. However, I think you can take it that goods in the quantity we have here would have undoubtedly been missed by now. However negligent the museum.

A round of applause followed this.

—Aye, said the Scottish voice : It's a clever enough point. But I still want to hear from Professor Garner. It's his book, and not a word have I heard from him. We knew one another well once; and I'll not go happy out of this room until he replies.

Stavros said : I understand.

Professor Garner received the microphone again and looked at it with a certain bewilderment. The Chairman bent over him, holding it and repeating the name of the questioner. Garner nodded. It struck Bernard that his skin had a pasty grey tinge. Nevertheless Garner stood up, clutching a small envelope and a few papers, and an unnecessary briefcase. The microphone was somewhere at his belly, so that even though he spoke with great vehemence he was completely inaudible.

—Speak up, came from several sections of the hall.

At this Garner looked embarrassed and bewildered, and did indeed attempt to do just that, shouting until the cords stood out in his neck, and the unhealthy look of his face turned from paste to plum-red.

Bernard could just make out a word or two, but could fit them into no kind of sense. The Chairman intervened at last, pulling the briefcase from Garner's awkward grasp, and pulling the microphone hand up to the level of Garner's lips.

—Not here to put about lies. Enough *lies* in the world already, Garner roared, like a lion released.

The sudden sound astonished everyone, but chiefly Garner, who fell silent, and sat down again, looking exhausted. It was at this point that a middle-aged lady in a hat from the back row, spoke up with perfect clarity; Professor Garner, will you tell us how much of this work was completed by your first wife?

8

—Take the keys, said Bernard : And go back to the
Garden House, will you?
Harriet stared incredulously.
—I've something to do, he explained.
—But what will I do there on my own? she asked in
astonishment.
—I don't know, it was your idea booking us at the bloody
place. You can sit at the bar and eat olives if you like.
—Bernard, said Harriet : I think you're behaving *very*
oddly. I wanted to mention it, last week; but I hoped it
was just some passing stress. Now I wonder! You know
darling, there's a very good friend of mine here who's
absolutely marvellous with problems of middle-aged men.
Bernard?
—Here. Catch. The car's over there, can you see it?
—Bernard! I haven't finished yet.

—May I cadge a lift? Bernard asked Professor Garner,
who greeted him with a certain cagey friendliness, as
Stavros was helping his legs into position at the front of
the car : Is there room in the back?
—Yeah, course, said Cressida : Come on in.
Stavros paused cautiously for a moment with his hand
on the car door : What did you make of it, Bernikins?
Think it went well?
Before Bernard could formulate a reply, Stavros leant
over and continued, in a much lower voice : The Professor

is all broken up. Thinks it was a failure. Be tactful, will you?

—What was all that about his wife?

—Yes. That's what he's blubbering about now, I should think. Well, get in.

Garner was sobbing in the front seat, without check or embarrassment. The saltwater ran down the grainy runnels of his cheeks, and funnelled itself into his nose and mouth. It was a noisy, uninhibited grief; an abandonment to choking and rumbling, that had dissolved all the muscle control in his face. As Stavros moved the driving seat backwards to accommodate his legs, Cressida bent forward and gently wiped the Professor's nose for him. He turned a face of misery towards her, nodding.

—Again, please.

—There, she said.

—*Worst* day of my life. *Worst*. Why should they mention her? *She* wasn't a scholar; just happened to *speak* Arabic. Malicious sods. Brought up in Cairo, nothing remarkable about that, is there?

Bernard was so surprised by the direction of Garner's dismay, he found himself saying: Brought up as a Moslem, was she?

—No. Jewish family. What's the use even trying to explain? he said: The woman never had an idea in her whole life. Just liked to help out, you know. Help me out.

And the sobbing mysteriously began again, starting from the shoulders and shaking the whole body.

—Should have been the happiest day of my life. Now it's all *tainted*. Tainted.

—Perhaps other things could have made it less than perfect? hinted Bernard.

Stavros caught his eye in the mirror: Where did you say you wanted dropping?

—Depends where you are going?

114

—Back to the village, said Cressida.
—Fine, said Bernard : That'll do me.

Bernard put one hand, rather squeamishly, on Cressida's knee. Instantly, he saw, he had her attention. She leant back; while the Professor went on snuffling quietly to himself, into a long pink roll of serrated tissue paper. Fascinated and appalled, Bernard let Cressida guide his hand upwards past her stocking tops, until he could feel the silk of her knickers. The knickers were a tremendous relief. Nevertheless, the troubled progress of his fingers continued as he spoke : The Press were there in force, Professor. I should think you'll be in every gossip column in the country.

—Well said Stavros sharply : *That* wasn't our intention. You're wrong anyway; most of the papers ran the story today. That's why we had such a large audience.

—My life's work, said the Professor.

—I think it went very well, said Bernard.

—Nobody understood, said Garner : They just didn't see the possibility of changing it all. All those terrible centuries of bloodshed and misery. Replacing them with an island of sanctuary and scholarship.

—Well, if it's any consolation, said Bernard rather hoarsely : It's an island that couldn't have lasted, could it?

—I beg your pardon?

—Couldn't have got through to the nineteenth century, said Bernard rather breathlessly.

Cressida had worked her knicker leg down so that he was making contact with a sharp textured nap of hair.

—We could talk about that, said the Professor who seemed rather cheered-up by the conversation : I've often wanted to discuss that aspect of things.

—You'll come in, won't you? said Cressida.

—Weren't we taking you somewhere? asked Stavros.

—That's all right, said Bernard: This is a special occasion.

—Take everyone in the library, Cressida, said Garner: All these spoons and so on had better go back in the safe. Whatever happened to? Ah yes. Where are you going, Stavros?

Stavros hesitated.

—Why – Bernard Hill, Garner said suddenly: I remember you now. Did you do well in your examination? You never wrote to say.

Bernard certainly remembered the library. It was unchanged from the days he had sat in it, under Garner's sleepy eye; in front of the same green, open-doored, coke-burning grate; with the same shelves of books covering the walls, the same velvet curtains, undrawn over giant Victorian windows into the rainy garden. The mantel, which in his memory had been larger, had four bottles standing on it and a small glass. Garner picked up the glass, sniffed it suspiciously, and then poured himself a generous tot of brandy. He then unexpectedly sat down in the only armchair in the room (another feature that had not changed), and motioned Bernard to find himself somewhere to sit also.

—I'll get some glasses, said Cressida, putting her tongue round her lips.

—Yes. Interesting, what you said about the nineteenth century. The nation state, I suppose you mean?

—Partly, said Bernard. His heart had begun to beat very fast, because both Stavros and Cressida had left the room, and he had his chance: Professor Garner, I must talk to you about your daughter.

—Cressy? Well, I, that's a manner of speaking. I mean she *may* and she may *not,* you know, winked Garner:

116

I've always looked after her. Her mother looked after my wife, you see. When she was ill. There was always some doubt, bound to be. And just as well, some days. If you follow me.

—But I mean *Miriam*, said Bernard : *Miriam*.

Garner lifted a tormented face out of his brandy glass and stared.

—Upstairs. She ought to see specialists. It's absurd. London. I could – I could *bring* someone. But why do you want to have her looked after *here*?

—Here? asked Garner slowly : She *can't* be here. The hospital said it was hopeless.

—But I've seen her, said Bernard, puzzled now : The room upstairs you had converted for her? Surely?

—Upstairs? Miriam?

The Professor's face collapsed altogether at the idea, and Bernard regretted speaking so harshly. Even as Stavros and Cressida returned to the room, he realized with absolute certainty that Garner knew nothing about the machinery or his unconscious daughter. For a moment, his own senses reeled at the possibility that Stavros had invented the whole set as a piece of theatre. Then he met Stavros' eyes.

—Now Bernard, chided Stavros : Can't have you *worrying* the professor, can we?

—We were only talking, said Bernard, mustering an alien jollity : Got a glass for me?

—*Upstairs?* said Garner.

—Rotten night, said Bernard quickly, meeting Cressida's side-on glance as he spoke : A brandy would do us all good, wouldn't it?

And the rain was blowing hard against the glass so that the loose branches of last year's creeper scratched against it like fingers.

Stavros accepted a glass in silence.

—Where you staying tonight? asked Cressida.

—I'm not booked in yet.

—We've got a lot of room.

—You're very kind.

—Upstairs? repeated Garner: Stavros, what's all this?

—Stay where you are, Bernard, won't you? said Stavros with unmistakable determination.

By ten thirty Harriet was sitting miserably on a single bed with pristine sheets folded back in a triangle, and the T.V. turned to B.B.C.2, trying hard not to cry. She had not enjoyed the expensive meal, eaten grimly alone two hours earlier; though she had allowed herself to have both the prawn cocktail and the consommé, and afterwards had chosen two slabs of fruit-covered cake from the trolley. Nothing had any taste. Her disappointment made her too miserable; as the evening wore on, it tightened her throat until she couldn't even finish her coffee. She had planned the whole excursion as a treat for Bernard and the point had gone out of it completely. She had intended it as a kind of offering, to lift him out of the depression she knew he fell into at the beginning of every academic year; an antidote to the drabness he seemed to fear closing in on him. And he had simply thrown the gift back in her face, rudely. He hadn't even seen the bathroom she thought, and picked up the two small printed pieces of soap to put them away neatly in her small case for the children. She had been amused at the American-style lavatory seat of paper, which declared that everything had been sterilized from all other human occupancy. She had liked the new blue bathtub, and looked forward to using it. And she'd bought a new nightdress. The thought of *that* made her flush with anger. Talking to the children on the phone, she had longed to rush off back to them at once, on a train. But the baby sitter had sounded so capably in control; and had been teaching her six-year old how to fold origami ducks. There really seemed no sense to going home and leaving the room totally unused. Though it *was* totally unused, she thought, staring at her own wooden face in the mirror, and asking herself: Where can he possibly be? Until this hour of night? And wherever it is, why doesn't he *telephone* and explain? You could always do that, there was always somewhere that had a telephone. He must know she'd be anxious.

Harriet had seen him go off in Garner's car, but couldn't imagine why. The man was an obvious fraud; the daughter was hideous; the whole occasion an embarrassment. It's true Harriet had *wanted* to come over and hear the lecture, originally because *The Guardian* had written about it; but really, the way they'd slanted the story, she'd thought it was something interesting and political about Arabs and Jews getting on perfectly well over centuries; and Zionism as some kind of European plot. She'd tried to get Garner's book from the library but it was always out, or she'd have realized at once it was just another piece of this horrible new interest in the occult that kept springing up everywhere. Well, Harriet didn't go to Church much any more, except when Mummy came to stay; but she still enjoyed singing the hymns. And she liked the good, washed feeling they gave you.

—Drained, you mean, Bernard said.

He could be very mean.

Anyway, she hated all these eclectic bits of Zen Buddhism, and Hindu *tantra* everyone used nowadays, as though there was something wrong with good old-fashioned Christianity.

—Which is bound to be true, if *any* of them are, she said.

—Why?

—Well it's just morally superior, she'd said triumphantly: isn't it?

Surely Bernard couldn't have been convinced into turning Moslem? Good heavens, what a terrible set of beliefs to be converted to. Whatever would the children say?

And where was he?

Harriet picked up the telephone directory, and looked down the considerable number of Garners for either an Octavius or a Professor, but no number was listed. After a moment's thought, she rang the College where he was presumably still a Fellow. The Porter's Lodge sounded unfriendly. It occurred to Harriet that she was probably not the first caller turned away that night by a flat voice saying : The Professor has asked us not to give his address to strangers. And he isn't on the phone.

Still, it established something. Harriet felt faintly cheered. Perhaps it had been difficult for Bernard to get in touch after all. She remembered now, Garner lived out in a village. She realized suddenly, with a sense of her own strength, that nothing could be easier than to find out the Professor's address. And the switchboard connected her immediately to the room of the friend who had written to her a fortnight ago.

—Dear Mary! Here I – we – are. In the hotel.

—Darling. Why didn't you drop in? Did you forget? What a shame!

—Well. We were both *so* tired. You know, what with the conference and term starting, Bernard just gets exhausted these days.

—Really? I saw him walking along the K.P. on Monday looking perky enough.

—Well, we're both tired now. I wonder if I could just trouble you for Professor Garner's address? asked Harriet abruptly : We want to drop him a letter. Just politeness, of course. He used to teach Bernard, you see.

—Hold on, I may still have it, though we don't send him supervisees any more.

—Because of his ideas?

—Nothing like that. He claims he hasn't time. Wait a minute. Yes. Here it is. Got a pencil?

—Ready, said Harriet.

An idea had been forming in her mind, and clarified itself as she wrote down the address. It had turned eleven, and in the ordinary way it would never have occurred to her to go out at such an hour, much less go to the expense of a taxi; now she could hardly wait to get Mary off the phone and set her plan into action.

She combed her hair, while Mary chattered on; and put a touch of red on her lips with one hand. Then she smiled at her reflection. She looked healthy and alert again. What was there to weep over? She was confident there was no evil in the world that could not be overcome by common sense.

9

—Yes, I've sold artifacts, said Stavros impatiently: If
you ever looked at the inventory in the safe you'd know.
It's all there. I'm not a petty thief. Or a vandal, come
to that; I made a point of selling nothing unique.
Bernard, *do* come away from the door. I can't answer
two people at once.

—But you *aren't* answering me, said Garner rather
shrewdly: I don't care *how* you financed an Intensive
Care Unit in my spare bedroom, I want to know *why*.

—I should have thought that was obvious, said Stavros,
shrugging.

Bernard began to walk up and down the pinewood
floor, agitatedly poking at a knot mark with his toe as
he went, cupping the brandy in the palms of his hands.
At the window he stopped and peered out. The rustling
of the leaves against the glass had changed to a kind of
continuous tapping; almost as if some lost spirit looked
for entrance. For a moment the thought clutched at him
and eclipsed the conversation, which continued.

—Perhaps. Or drink and drugs together, I don't know,
Stavros was saying: I hope you aren't accusing me of
inducing the coma, Professor.

It was a branch, Bernard supposed, broken and hanging loose. When the noise began again, he would surely
see a loose fibre or two swinging in the wind.

—People can only dream what they know, said Stavros:
Cressida could never find herself in the city, could she?

It really was the only way to prove anything, don't you see that?

Then Bernard turned away from the window for a moment, appalled by the callous precision of what was being said, and missing the next rattle of taps on the glass in a fury of unbelieving indignation.

—Do you mean to admit you're keeping Miriam in that state? For your own purposes?

—No, I'm keeping her alive, that's all, said Stavros, impatiently.

—I hope you won't object to me questioning the nurses, said Bernard, consciously pompous, though still for some reason afraid of Stavros' challenge.

—I certainly do at this hour of night.

—Why?

Professor Garner stared from one face to the other: I feel terrible, he said, sitting down suddenly.

—What about some food? said Cressida: There are three eggs. I could put a bit of milk with them, and some dried onions.

—Doesn't attract me, I must confess, said Stavros.

—It's disgusting, said Garner: What about the freezer? You only stocked up last week. Filled it with birds and meat, didn't you?

—Yeh, well. All that stuff needs unfreezing, though, said Cressida: Bit late to be standing in the kitchen pouring kettles of water over frozen chicken pieces.

—There were chops and steaks, said Garner querulously: *They're* quick enough for you aren't they?

—Let *me* help, said Bernard.

Cressida had a huge French cook's knife, and was trying to worry a layer of frozen meat out of the hot water.

—Let me, said Bernard: You don't need that hideous weapon.

—Oh, *don't* say that! I only just got it. Green Shield stamps, said Cressida proudly.

—What's Garner so upset about, anyway? Do you know? I thought *you* made an extraordinary witness, said Bernard truthfully: Frying pan somewhere?

—Here.

—What about salad?

—There's a few tomatoes.

—Plates? Bernard looked around: Cooking oil?

—Aren't you domestic? teased Cressida: Oh Garner's *always* weeping on, don't you know? Makes you sick really. All that money and whatever he wants.

—Can you remember his wife?

—No. But me Mum never liked her. Said she was too lady-like, and no reason for it, being what she was.

—What did she ever see in Garner then?

—Ask him. I don't think she ever liked it here. Well, except the green house. She planted herbs and vegetables and that peach tree. Shall I tell you a funny thing? Miriam told me to water it, and it's not dead? Anyway, there's masses of her stuff upstairs, said Cressida, coming up behind Bernard and pressing her shape into his buttocks: Coffers of junk.

—Mind, said Bernard: This oil is dangerous. What sort of stuff? Oh, *blast*. You have to seal the juices in, said Bernard, unconsciously quoting Harriet.

—I'm sorry. Are you hurt? I could show you her notebooks if you like. Can you read Arabic? Or Spanish? There aren't many in English you see. Have you burnt your thumb?

—Think I'll be all right, said Bernard: Yes. I can manage Spanish.

—Tell you what, said Cressida: I don't think Stavros trusts you. I'd better bring all of it down now, hadn't I?

—*That's* a good girl, said Bernard, reaching for her arse with a free hand.

—Rotten the way we don't ever get any time, complained Cressida, as she went.

They found Stavros and Garner deep in conversation. Stavros said: From your point of view I think it's clear enough. We should have gone for the mountain tribes. Latin will never conquer the mountains. Those *massifs* will always be hostile. That's where your civilization could have hidden out. Whole mountains could have resisted for years, I can't think why it was never tried. Or perhaps it was. Cities are always corrupt, look what's happened to urban America. You have to go on to the hilltops to find dissidents. Aberrant cults always make for them. We could have made a *true* magic mountain.
—Haven't we had enough of those? said Bernard: Have a plate, Stavros.
—Thank you. You say that, because, Bernie, you're a natural creature of flatlands, said Stavros: Pliant, well-meaning and docile. We need a separate religious geography for mountain people.
—I'm dogged though, said Bernard.
Garner, who had by now eaten his tomatoes and half his steak ferociously, suddenly put down the plate on the floor and gave a low moan.
—Esther, he said: My poor Esther. I treated her badly; didn't I? I've been wicked. I've been a wicked man. And then he began to weep.

   Less harrowed by the old man's tears than in the car, Bernard looked up questioningly at Stavros; it was Cressida however who replied: Esther was that wife. *You* know.
—Esther, Esther, sobbed Professor Garner.
—Look out, you'll break the plate.
—How many years was it, how many years, *centuries* it was, *must* have been, since her family were forced out of

125

Toledo? And they kept that name: *Toledano.* That's what *took* me into their shop in the first place. It was just an ordinary trinket shop, otherwise. Nothing rich or splendid. But you know what the old man still wore round his neck? *Keys.* To the family house.

—In Cairo you mean?

—*Keys* to their *old* house. The house the family left behind centuries ago in Toledo, don't you follow? Garner shook his head: What a memory! What a *persistence*! And all the daughters spoke Spanish, old Spanish, a real old fourteenth-century Castilian which you'll not find anyone speaking in Spain today. Imagine that.

He wept again.

—And I brought her here. To this country. Well it killed her. Because I regretted it, and she was miserable and lonely here, and I didn't care. She sort of scared me, because she believed it all. Everything. That's why, I swear it. The only reason I had to take the child away from her. Because of her terrible *believing* I didn't want Miriam to be a part of such an unhappy persistent people. Such a centuries-enduring memory. I wanted her to grow up free of that. Can you understand? After all, what good did it ever bring any of them?

He spluttered into a yellow handkerchief, the colour of snuff.

—And what difference did it make. Whatever I did? The dream was waiting.

—All very interesting, said Bernard: But how do you know what Miriam is dreaming?

—It's always the same, said Garner gloomily. And belched.

Miriam had feared prison; but they were only in another room of the house. Luis' room, she thought. The walls were decorated with gilded leathers and precious fabrics

126

ornamented with raised tulips. On a low copper table stood four glasses, a flagon of water, a ceramic bowl and a spoon of rock crystal.

—So Ibn Ezra has adopted you for his daughter, said Ramon taking fruit from the bowl thoughtfully.

Miriam said : I haven't accepted his offer.

—Clever of you. As it turns out.

—Where have you taken Esther?

—To be questioned.

—How?

Ramon raised his eyebrows and yawned : Does it matter? Come here.

Miriam hesitated. The familiarity of the white face and glittering eyes was for the moment inexplicable. She obeyed him, however.

—Lie here, in the straw. Lower.

She did as he said.

—Lift your skirt.

Miriam hesitated, and then raised her long silk robe above her knee.

But Ramon said roughly : No. Pull it underneath you; don't be so chaste. Up to your thighs.

Miriam obeyed. Then Ramon casually put out his hand, laid it between her bare legs, and with his thumb opened the softness of the flesh between them.

—Look at me, he commanded.

She looked up into eyes which she suddenly saw were without joy, or lust. Then the door opened. At the lintel she saw Luis. Miriam made a move to rise, revolted at the sight of his full under-lip swelling with saliva. Ramon's hand, however, continued to hold her down; and he said, even as his thumb caressed her clitoris : Here you are, Luis. For you.

And for a moment, Miriam expected the large, wet-mouthed man to stride over and take her on command; rather to her surprise, the expectation was almost pleasurable because of the strong hand that held her pinioned to the floor, and the indifferent eyes that clearly waited to watch the performance. Luis however, turned, unexpectedly aside from the opportunity.

—No, Ramon. I've no heart for it. Your friends from Cluny have questioned Esther harshly. She is crying. Why? She suffers enough Ramon. And where is the harm in white magic? My son is well, isn't he?

—Miracles are not important.

Reflectively he looked down at the girl on the floor and lifted his hand. Miriam spun away from him, her cheeks burning.

—My job here is to teach you people to understand shame. You can comfort your wife, Luis. Later. First take these documents, which I want you to sign. Here is the first.

He held the paper out towards Luis, who waved a despairing hand of unwillingness even to think of the matter. Miriam was therefore able to read both of them.

Repudiation of Marriage after consummation

Luis, son of Ibn-Idhari, solemnly renounces his wife Esther, daughter of Ibn Ezra, having consummated his marriage with her. He has had no intercourse with her for a full menstrual period. Witnesses for the said Luis, son of Ibn-Idhari, in full knowledge of allegations made against him, refute them outright and testify that he is in good health, and full possession of his faculties.

Given this   day   of the year

Authorization of a wife for her husband to take a concubine.

Esther, daughter of Ibn Ezra, calls on the undersubscribed witness to testify that her husband Luis, son of Ibn Ezra, has sought her permission to have a concubine; since if he take a concubine without her permission she can in law sell or keep the concubine at her discretion. The wife hereby authorizes him to take a concubine, renouncing her rights in the matter freely and of her own will.

Witnessed by

—She was looking for her sister, that was all. Her poor *sister,* Luis said, his eyes wet : Why should I do this?
—Go on, said Ramon : Do as I say.
His own gaze was hooded. Miriam watched closely.
—Well, I will take them with me, said Luis uncertainly. Then he left, saying no more.

—You are a northerner, said Miriam uncertainly.
—Yes, there are many of us. Princes, monks, and labourers; we pour south every day now and bring in the customs of the rest of Europe. And Spain is part of that great Europe, though she does not yet understand herself.
—And you want her to burn in joining it, exclaimed Miriam.
—Burn? On the contrary. I want to make sure no soul will be lost in the fire, said Ramon, laughing.
—And you support this invasion in the name of which God? demanded Miriam violently.
—Only in the name of the understanding of Sin, said

Ramon quietly : I do not think the people of Toledo have been taught about the Fall of man. They have read too many books and too much Science and they think themselves in Eden. But we are *not* in Eden, and men should know the truth.

—So you plan to police men's *souls,* do you? said Miriam ironically.

—For their good.

—And Luis' good? What good are you doing with him? You are debauching him. Why?

—These great families of Toledo have to be punished. They are too proud altogether. They boast of the purity of their line; claim David as an ancestor. It is *necessary* to corrupt them.

—For their good?

—Yes. To give them a true sense of their own sinfulness. So they may be saved.

—I wonder why, said Miriam : You are not afraid for your own soul? I would be.

Ramon smiled : Do I seem afraid?

His smile disturbed her deeply. Miriam muttered : I am beginning to feel ill. Will you let me go now?

—Not yet. There are things I want to know. First. How do you understand the treatment of wounds?

—I can't remember, said Miriam huskily.

—Too evasive. Answer directly. How? By what means? Books?

—I can't remember. It is common knowledge.

—Where?

Miriam fell into a sullen silence. It was as if for the first time, she could see the horizon of her sense of the past and present clearly. It was no longer a matter of remembering confusedly as if in a dream, how she had come to be in this situation. She could feel an edge to her knowledge. A terrifying precipice.

—If only I *could* remember, she muttered.

And suddenly she was convinced that if she could reach the edge of her thought and look over, she would be freed from more than this questioning.

Meanwhile Ramon continued to speak.

—The Church will put pressure on the King soon enough. Then the tanners will hang their skins to dry on your gravestones, and vagabonds will come to rape your children. Your people will learn to hide and cringe; but we shall find them. By their very hiding and their cringing. Tell me. Who are your mother and father?

—My mother? echoed Miriam: I can't remember her. If only I could remember. Something. Some gentle reproach. Any word or sign. Why *have* I no memory of her?

—Your father then?

No, she said silently, don't confuse me: here is what I must remember and have forgotten; have known and forgotten.

—Let me think, she cried aloud.

Ramon asked several more questions and then became bored and impatient.

—Luis will put you in another room, he said.

Green wings   silent voices of alarm. Over her, a solicitous head   tight green rubberized skull-cap   no lips green mask.

—Look at the dials.

—The dials. The dials.

The stone-room was cold and wet as if the rains of winter had got into it. Miriam coughed continuously, one uncontrolled bout running into the next; barely leaving time for desperate intakes of breath. She choked often. Sometimes on vomit, and sometimes on a film of stick chest secretions and burning drops of nose snot.

Where and when is this winter, she thought, and this cold city? On some hostile *massif*, a harsh plateau? She had never imagined such a ferocity of chill, eating into her bones. I shall die, she thought. And still I don't understand. What I am doing in this small room, facing north? Why have I been abandoned here? What *is* it I have to remember?

Mother, she called, Mother. Where are you? I remember. Your soft brown hair and small teeth. I remember your death. The leaves were all gone from the high boughs and they lay brown on the grass in deep piles under the beeches. And I was crying. I held the hand of a giant with broad red cheeks and black hair; my nurse, was she? Full-lipped, hard boned, hard as nails, a bit deaf. But you were gentle and your lips were tender and your teeth when you smiled were like the white seed teeth of Esther's son. Who taught me to forget you for so long? I think I forgot you even when you were alive.

Time passed. Miriam dozed. When she woke with a start, facing another way, as her eyes cleared she observed the fourth wall of her cell. How was it she had never observed the door was open? Had she been too ill even to move her eyes round the bare white walls? Was she no prisoner but her own? She was cold; sitting upright made her heart pound. She was dizzy and her head ached. As soon as she felt the stone floor under her bare feet, she was seized, as if a giant hand had scrunched up the tissue of her lungs, with a paroxysm of coughing. They can well risk leaving the door open, she thought, if I can't even cross the room to it. And then she leant back, covered with the perspiration of effort; a cold perspiration that left her weak and trembling.

When she could open her eyes again, there was a dark figure at the door, a silent figure with a covered face. Miriam seemed to recognize the quiet gesture of the beckoning hand, and the fine fingers that pulled a green head-scarf closer over the lower half of her face. Whoever it was, the hand threw an embroidered shawl towards Miriam's bed, and then the figure was gone.

Miriam's fingers felt the warmth in the wool like the touch of an animal. To have wool round her shoulders was like a warm arm, steadying her. She tried again. This time it was possible to walk. To go through the door. Even to walk up the shallow winding steps into the dazzle of light; with waking hope, she felt the new warmth of air at the level of the earth's surface. The contrast in temperature was as extraordinary as leaving a cave. Gradually her shivering ceased. She followed the rooms as they opened into one another, until she looked through and saw Ibn Ezra and her heart began to bang again. She had to lean against the wall, for support.

Through a door she could see Ibn Ezra's face was calm as he went on writing. She could hear his pen. By his side stood a shining pot of coffee; but he was too absorbed in his work even to drink from the small cup he had already poured. Miriam longed for the hot drink; and at the same time she was puzzled. He seemed so at ease. If Ramon had ever taken control of this house, there was no sign of it. Ibn Ezra's face was tranquil. When occasionally he saw something in the documents he was studying that displeased him, he scratched at it with his pen, and frowned with concentration. She could hear the noise of the pen over the surface of the parchment. It surprised her, in a way, that her own wheezing presence was not instantly sensed by him. And surely days must have passed. Had he not noticed her absence? Was he indifferent to it? Or had he forgotten all about her?

There Ibn Ezra sat squat, and cross-legged and intense; his reflection caught in beaten silver behind him. His tough black hair, his dark face, his disproportionately powerful neck and arms. If she moved a step or two to the right she would meet her own reflection in the same mirror. But Miriam felt afraid to do it. She wasn't sure why. Was she afraid to find her hair grey? Or her beauty despoiled? No, it wasn't that.

It came to her that she was afraid of being invisible. Ibn Ezra's face was unclouded by her memory; she could be sure not to exist in his mind. But did she truly exist in this ante-chamber? She felt voiceless. If she called into the room, would he hear? Had she the power of noise? The thought frightened her. She wondered whether if she called a desperate warning he would hear anything. Would the real air move? If she stood before a mirror, would she displace light? She felt no certainty of it.

She had a warning to cry, but she was afraid to put it to the test. Not afraid of Ibn Ezra's reaction; not suspicious of him; but afraid he would not hear or see her. That he would not lift his head. That she would be like someone crying on the moon. As if she occupied a soundless planet, without reverberation. She was afraid of the mirror, in case it gave back no reflection. The sensation in her limbs was unpleasant. It was like dissolving. Not as if the world about her was losing solidity, but herself. She was dwindling. She was disappearing. She was almost gone altogether; soon it must be as if she had never existed.

And still she wished to call out with great passion, such a prophecy of disaster she must have burnt like a torch shouting it. But it was too late. She had become a ghost, only a ghost; she understood herself so. And her throat dried, and she called nothing, but passed by looking for no-one; and no-one passed her, as she quietly searched for a way out onto the street.

In the library, Garner solemnly chomped on his food again ruminating: I've no excuse. Mind you, I don't say her father was a rich man, but when he said here is your dowry, I didn't expect a copper copy of those useless bloody keys. I mean I opened the velvet parcel after the ceremony and I couldn't believe it; the whole family kissed me and said now I was one of them. I remember saying well, they are lovely. I've always wanted to own a house in Spain for holidays. And they laughed.

Bernard said: In her trunk, were they? Well, Cressida can lift that down. She's stronger than she looks, you know.

Cressida went red and glared with fury at him.

—Why d'you say that? she said: I think that's rotten. Why are you telling *them*?

Stavros looked puzzled: Bernie?

And Garner stopped eating in mid-bite: Is something going on?

Cressida said: I thought fat men were different. Well, now I know better, don't I?

—Is it in the conservatory? asked Bernard gently: Please get it.

—What's this now? said Stavros: What are you after? Garner's always meandering on like that about something or other. What do you imagine you've hit upon?

—It's a sort of hunch, said Bernard modestly: The trouble with you, Stavros, is you aren't a historian.

10

—I had another padlock made, said Cressida : Well, that's easy enough to do.

It was a small leather trunk. Not, as Bernard had half imagined, a treasure chest with copper bands and multiple locks or chains over it.

—What's worrying you now? Stavros asked the Professor.

Garner bit his handkerchief; Cressida opened the case; and a subtle spicy odour came from a mantilla of silk at the top of the trunk. Underneath was a small box of about the size of a travelling bag. It contained a few small, carefully wrapped pieces of jewellery; a brooch, a bracelet, some rings and the bunch of copper keys. Underneath a layer of cloth, Bernard saw six or seven schoolbooks, all bound together neatly with a piece of silvery gift-ribbon.

—It doesn't seem right, said Garner nervously : I *never* felt it was right to look.

—No doubt, Stavros said : However. What's all the fuss? Meanwhile Cressida's long jumpy fingers were at the ribbon in any case.

—Stop, said Garner covering his face.

—Why don't you see? She's read them before ! said Bernard roughly : Idiots ! Both of you. It's so clear. She's had them out *dozens* of times. Look at her.

—I like this one *best*, said Cressida, smiling : This is happy.

—Look in the trunk, said Bernard impatiently : Go on. Garner and Stavros exchanged incredulous glances.

Bernard picked up one of the exercise books, while Stavros and Garner scrabbled into the bottom of the trunk and brought out several spoons and a flagon all lovingly wrapped in scarves of fine design.

Bernard looked up briefly to say: You mustn't blame Cressida, you know, because you put her in a spot, didn't you? She did her best.

And then he read on.

Of the three Jerusalems, Toledo was the most beautiful, they say. Perhaps; but I was happiest with my sister. In Abu Tor. She lived alone, in a small flat with a balcony, and at night it was cool. We ate pitta with olives, hard boiled eggs and tomatoes in the morning, and drank lemon tea. Such a happy year. One day she showed me the desert. If you leave town you see the Bedou dressed in black and herding goats. There are deep ravines but the Bedou never pitch tent there, because the ravines flood in winter. In the desert you don't sweat. I liked it. We walked together up the white sandy road alongside Arab women carrying bunches of coriander in their woven baskets. When we came to the oasis she showed me green fruit filled with fluff, and I *gagged* on the thought of it. But there were also acacia trees, and a pump of water, resinous trees all about us, and shade. I remember the deeply-ridged desert hills, with caves in them, and the white pebbled path we climbed together to David's pool. We both put our faces into the water and drank. Yes, we drank blessed cold water from those yellow hills, like a miracle. And then after drinking, we jumped into the water in full dress; and we laughed because our clothes dried so quickly except for a pleasant dampness between our breasts and legs.

Yes I was happy with my sister. I shall not see her again now. I am too ill and poor to visit her, and she will not miss me. She is too busy. She has her own shop and doesn't intend to marry. She likes the old Arab market where the stalls are piled high with fruit, meat, jewellery, and small tables. I pointed to the streets of filth that lay behind, and the flies; but nothing has ever perturbed her. —Aren't you afraid? I asked.

She is never afraid, not even when the youths throw stones along the small pebbled streets, and call her *Witch, Jewess, whore*. It's all the same, she said: If you dodge the stones.

Here in England the rains come all year long, and no-one talks to me. If they call me rude names, it is quietly so I never hear it. My husband takes me nowhere, though I have tried hard to learn the language. I spend hours alone. I wish I enjoyed being alone. My sister always said it was the greatest luxury a woman could have. I don't understand that.

Sometimes my husband hates me. I don't know why. I try to help him. Sometimes I think he is stupid; he tries to make Arabic say what he wants; and he never listens to me. I know my ways annoy him, but I don't know how to change myself. I no longer use garlic or sesame seeds or olive oil in our food. I eat what he eats. When he bothers to come home. I know my ways are foreign. He used to like my ways. But not here in this town.

They say my father had a Pasha's house once.

My baby is round and beautiful. Octavius said she looked like his family; and I was so happy to nurse her, so full of love and joy; I sang with joy, looking at the thick black hair, and the huge brown eyes. So I didn't argue with him. But she looks like my sister. It was summer when she was born, and I could walk outside with a pram; people stopped to look at her, she was so perfect. I was glad she was a girl. Octavius had been worrying about that. He didn't want any mention of circumcision. How can you brand such a misfortune in a child's flesh? he said. And I prayed to God it would never come to that quarrel.

I gave her the sister's name of one of my ancestors who was a poet in Spain. We argued about it; but luckily someone from his college told him how *The Times* had counted names again, and Sarah and Rebecca and Deborah were quite popular. So he agreed. He'd wanted to call her after a lady in Jane Austen, so I let him give her that name too. But she will be Miriam. I am sure of that.

She spoke early and now she can walk too. I watch her in the garden. Octavius delights in her. He takes her down at night to show her off to the guests. Only I am never taken down to meet them. Too sick, he says. But I know it is my pale yellow skin; my dark sunken eyes he wants to hide. I make people uneasy. Now I can read the papers, I have learnt what has been happening in Europe, so I understand Octavius better. He tells my friends I am Egyptian. I don't mind, it is true. My father always said so. I remember my father teaching me a poem from Spain, it was sad. I recited it to Octavius. Such a sad poem. But it made him angry.

> I have said the Credo,
> I have prayed to the pot of fat pork
> I have heard Masses and I have prayed
> I have prayed with devotion
> And I have counted beads
> But I have never been able to lose
> The name of an old Jew.

Antonio de Montoro wrote it, to Isabella, when they were only beginning, the bad times. My father says, we left Toledo for Italy first, and then Salonica. We moved often, and always further and further away. With our songs and stories.

So I remember my family house, and its garden. The citrus fruit, and the pools of water, and the shade of trees. Every flower was a sign of work and love; and water was holy. Here in this country, Nature does all the work; the trees live without help. Who can love water in this rain?

It isn't true that Miriam looks like Octavius' family. They are northern people. She will never laugh with their voice. But when I said they were loud-mouthed, Octavius shouted at me. To me they do not seem like women of culture, but fishwives; with their swearing and smoking. But evidently they are acceptable here. Octavius calls me prim. He says: They are good English middle-class and I should learn their manners. What manners? I ask him. And he teaches me. Dress *quietly,* he says, in beige or brown; and wear tweed when you go out. It is a disguise he wants me to wear. I prefer to stay in my room. From my window I can watch Miriam in the garden. Every day I pray she will grow up free. I want her to wear copper necklets and green agate, and dance with joy when she wants. As if she had truly crossed the Red Sea out of Egypt and could stand on the shore singing in triumph.

Already she has grace and balance beyond the manner of the children she plays with. I watch her walk along the branch of a tree without fear. She holds herself without pride, but with great certainty.

Only one thing I fear, she will become world-lost and world-drowned. Like my own sister who had fine thoughts too young, and used to lie by my side as a child with her spirit floating off like a balloon, whatever I said. I used to fear she would never come back to me. And now she lives alone and enjoys her loneliness. But I want Miriam to marry. It is true I have not been happy, but I remember there was great love between my parents, and I believe, even now, in the possibility of love between man and woman. Even now I could love Octavius, if he could forgive me. Forgive me for being what I am, which I cannot change.

My father told me so many legends. I like to remember them. His stories of Toledo are as clear as dreams to me. I see the city like an island in the sun.

The town was biscuit coloured, seen from the road beside the Tagus. The long horizon of eroded mountains lay behind, bare and uninhabited; even though aromatic plants grew on the upper slopes. At the roadside, exhausted by hunger and thirst, a family lay sheltering as best they could from the sun and waiting for the heat to drop from its afternoon height.

—What a cheating bitch, said Stavros : My god, I'll kill her. Cressida said : How did I cheat? I got what *you* asked for. I never pretended I could do what *he* said. Did I? *You* cheated me. Putting me to sleep every time. I never once enjoyed it. Every morning, there was semen on the sheets, I could smell it on my fingers, but you never let me enjoy it once. You could have *once,* couldn't you? I mean that was really not much to ask, was it? Drink this you said. Do this. Lie there. How did I cheat? Didn't I do what you said?

Stavros breathed deeply, his face tense with anger, patiently : You only have made me look the most gullible man in the Western Hemisphere. That's all. If this gets out I'll never be able to open my mouth in public again.

He looked at Bernard broodily.

—Not that they'll believe *you,* he said under his breath : Bernard they might believe. But not you. In fact, apart from Garner, he's more or less our only credible prosecution witness. Isn't he?

—What are you doing?

—I'm looking for that rather elegant Victorian antique doorstop, said Stavros.

Bernard looked up innocently.

At which moment, the front doorbell went, with a loud, persistent resonance. It was a noise which puzzled all four of them.

—If that is the Police, little Bernie, said Stavros : I shan't be at *all* friendly about it. I think I'll just hold you here for a few moments while we find out. Answer the door, Cressida.

Saying this, Stavros put his hand across Bernard's throat, and drew him up on tip-toe flat against his own chest.

—Japanese war hold, he explained : Very dangerous if you wriggle. California's a useful place, Bernie, you should get about more.

Bernard felt the blood pounding in his ears, but could not utter a sound. He shuffled one leg backward, absurdly, trying for a half-remembered childhood Judo hold.

—Now then, said Stavros : Stop it.

Bernard caught Cressida's eye. She looked thoughtful. It came to him with a certain relief that she didn't want Stavros to damage him, in spite of his treachery.

The bell sounded again. Bernard sighed as he thought how their anxieties were only too hopelessly without foundation. Why *hadn't* he had the intelligence to tell anyone where he was going? Nevertheless someone was at the door.

—Yeah, who are you?

He could hear Cressida; but the other voice was inaudible.

—You've made a mistake, good night, Cressida said woodenly.

Neither Stavros nor Bernard could catch a reply, but whoever stood outside was more determined than usual. Fascinated, Stavros and Bernard peered into the hall together and saw a firm, flat shoe at the end of a neat ankle placed bravely in the door. Cressida opened her side of the door a little way with the intention of giving the invading foot a vicious blow, but some firm, rounded body was too quick for her.

—Shut the door, ordered Stavros immediately releasing Bernard and staring. Bernard also stared at Harriet with mixed feelings.

—Now you have the facts, said Stavros: You see. It
can't be long either way. The brain patterns are scattering. The dreams are breaking up. It's ending.

Garner said: Help me. Oh, I can't stand it, Cressida.
Take me away. God oh god god. I can't bear it. Why
should such a horrible thing happen to me?

—To *you*? said Bernard: It *isn't* happening to you.

—Bernie! said Cressida, with a kind of warning in her
voice. Then Harriet spoke almost her first word since she
had insisted on seeing Miriam: I notice not one of these
nurses speak English. How do you know they're qualified
to handle all this machinery? How do we know one of
you won't come along in the middle of the night and
throw a switch? I think it's all very peculiar.

Bernie, very conscious of Stavros' hand on his shoulder,
said: Darling, I don't think you've quite understood.

—You mean you think we should just go away? And
leave her like this? With these people?

Stavros' hand pressed warningly at the base of Bernie's
neck.

—I agree with you entirely in principle, said Bernie
guardedly: But what do you suggest? At the moment?

For the first time Harriet took in the position of
Stavros' hand and the colour of Bernie's face.

—Are you threatening my husband?

Stavros made a deprecating face: I'm really very sorry
about this.

Garner shook his head: I don't really see how we can
keep them here, Alexander. I mean people will notice.

This young man has to earn his living. Anyway, what on earth should we do with them?

Stavros said: Well, now. There's no need to discuss that in here, surely.

Harriet said: Well. I'm not moving.

Cressida came forward and said to Harriet nodding toward Bernard: You his wife?

—Yes, I am.

—What do you want to help *her* for? He likes her, I think.

—Good heavens, look at her. How can you ask? I'm sure he did or does, said Harriet with difficulty: like her.

—Yeah. Well. She did let me have a dress once, muttered Cressida: I suppose.

—Now, Cressy, said Stavros: Nothing bad is happening in here. I explained all that. These nurses are *helping* Miriam. That's the point of all this machinery.

—Yeah, you said.

—Why don't you just let these people go back to their hotel? said Garner.

—Because, said Stavros patiently: They will immediately get in touch with the Police, half the University, and the National Press.

—Surely not?

Harriet said: No. Because I've no intention of leaving this room until someone calls a doctor I can trust.

—Do you know, said Garner: I'm inclined to agree with this sensible young woman?

—You senile old twit, said Stavros: If it doesn't matter to you what happens next, it does to me.

Harriet smiled, her most complacent cat-like smile: It's not really going to be so easy for you, is it? After all.

The intruders made shadows on the ceiling. It seemed to Miriam now that she had seen their shape many times,

145

shadows on the ceiling, always rippling as if under water;
There was a river in her memory, a green river, and the
shadows were green also. Like the silk that the figure at
the lintel pulled round her features. Green.

If she shut her eyes she was under a river bridge, with
the waterlight playing on the old stones above her, and
damp rising in green moss with the overhanging curve.
She had not been alone all the time then; there had been
voices outside the room, she was sure now; other lives
went on outside her room, and occasionally they lapped
into her room, now she thought about it three figures
came to tend her often. Perhaps a man also? And a
woman with peaches and a huge knife, and a strange tic.
Miriam could still see her slicing every peach, with those
nervous jerking hands; terrified that the knife would
slip, and the irritable knobbly fingers would be hurt. Her
own eyes were so red-hot she thought longingly of cool
juice, even as she watched the knife anxiously, slicing and
slicing at the fruit. And feared for the poor grotesque
hands.

—Eh, Eh, the woman said.

But she seemed unharmed.

And now the green river was sticky and no longer a
comfort; it ran with a foul stench deeper and over both
of them. And it was hotter than the air or Miriam's blood.
If she could only burst out of the fathoms it lay over her.
But to swim up was as hard as flying would be.

Harriet said : What's that noise?

—It's the wind, said Bernard : The creepers against the
glass again. I don't know. The whole bloody house
creaks.

—But there aren't any windows, they're all blocked off.
Garner said : She's right. It's the machinery. It's going
off. Look. There's a red light coming on over there.

Stavros, what does that mean? A red light.

—What language do they speak? said Bernard: Come on, Stavros. Harriet said, in a very English voice: *Qu'est-ce que vous croyez soit mal dans les machines?* Bernard said, in rather uncomfortable Spanish: What's happening? Is there any danger?

Stavros said: They're Indian, you sap.

—Oh, said Garner: Which part, I wonder?

And fell into immediate conversation.

Words flew between them, first in sentences and then appalling monosyllables. Then Garner sat down against the wall and began to sob.

—What? What? said Bernard: Come on you silly old man, if it isn't too late. What are they *saying* to you?

—They're leaving. They've only been paid up till tonight. The red light, said Garner: is a power failure. Look at that green rubber. It isn't fluttering up and down any more.

—There must be something we can do.

—We could take that horrible tube out of her mouth, said Harriet: Maybe she can breathe herself. I doubt if anyone's been giving her much of an opportunity to try.

—I think they must have been, said Bernard: Or how could anyone listen to her rambling? And you *have* been listening, haven't you, Stavros?

—You bloody fool. Keep still, said Stavros: Is that clear?

Bernard saw that Cressida's arms were trembling, and that her face had its own peculiar shake in it; as if her whole soul were about to fly apart. Her mouth, especially the flesh of her under lip, trembled. Only her eyes which had become round and childlike again were very still.

She was wearing the blue plastic apron with a red heart pocket on the hip, which she had put on to protect her clothes in the kitchen. Bernard saw her hand go secretly into the red heart sewn-on patch pocket; saw that her eyes fixed on Stavros' throat. He watched, hypnotized, as her hand moved about in the pocket, and she moved closer.

She licked her lips. Bernard knew the gesture. It was nervously erotic. At the same time he remembered the French cook's knife.

The nurses in their green masks had gone like spirits. Some dials still turned; some instruments still moved. Bernard wondered if any damage done was reversible. It seemed to him that Miriam's face had deepened in colour.

—Stavros, said Cressida, in a strange high-pitched and rising voice : You're not to hurt *him*. See?

—Garner, yelled Bernard : Look !

Miriam opened her eyes while Stavros and Cressida were arguing. She stared up and sideways. She looked puzzled. She could not move her arms, or her head. To the side, she watched a green-rubber structure in a plastic case. She became conscious of tubes in her intimate ducts. She could not speak for the machinery about her mouth. But she could hear voices, and a continuous monotone of crying.

—I've never heard anything so stupid, said Stavros.

—No. You're a *real* sod, agreed Cressida.

—Oh shut up, said Stavros : What does it matter? Bernard, stay where you are.

—What is he afraid of I wonder? asked Harriet : She must be all right, Bernard. Or he wouldn't care.

Miriam thought : Have I swum up through all the fathoms of that green river into another nightmare? For a moment she hesitated. Her whole body hesitated.

—I'm going to risk it, said Bernard : She can see me.

—What about the clamp?

—Don't move, said Stavros : I forbid you to move.

—Why? said Cressida.

Garner said : Stavros. Please be reasonable.

Stavros' hand tightened on Bernard's neck again : She's dying, you idiots, he said : She's bound to. Why are you behaving so childishly? Her eyes are open but still. No eye-movements. No dreams. That's what it means. It's ending.

—What you mean is, you want it to end, said Cressida : It's a real kink with you. Preferring people unconscious. Now just take your hand off *his* neck.

—Because you say so? asked Stavros amused.

—Yeh, that's right, said Cressida rather breathlessly.

Stavros laughed. So up came her hand with the French cook's knife and plunged into Stavros' back, just below the shoulder blade. To everyone's astonishment he went down instantly.

—Good heavens, said Garner : Now we'll *have* to get a doctor. At this Harriet began to laugh hysterically.

Blood began to pour from Stavros' lips.

Then Bernard moved across to Miriam. With trembling hands he began to undo the clamp. Her mouth opened. Everyone listened.

—She's breathing, said Harriet, tearfully.

—There now, said Cressida : I thought as much.

12

—I suppose she must still feel rather strange, said Harriet.

—Yes.

—What do you want me to tell the children?

—Must you tell them anything? Couldn't I just be on a kind of sabbatical? asked Bernard.

Harriet said: Darling, I am *not* very modern I'm afraid. When I talked about it with other wives, you know, whose husbands were being silly with students all the time, it wasn't the same. I thought I wouldn't mind. But I do. I'm sorry.

—I think you're being marvellous.

—Do you? asked Harriet, more hopefully.

—Letting me go, I mean.

—Yes. I see.

—Tell the children what you like.

Harriet said: I wish I understood. That's the trouble. She's still ill, isn't she? Where will you go? Can you cope?

—At first she kept talking about flying off to Cairo and finding what's left of her mother's family, but it turns out they've moved to France recently. I think I can organize a trip to *France*, you know.

—Have you told her everything?

—About Stavros? No, admitted Bernard.

—Shouldn't you?

—The doctors all advised against it.

—She's bound to hear though. Isn't she?

—Not in France, she isn't. I'm not sure they even reported the case.

—Must be the only country that didn't then. Oh dear, Bernard, said Harriet: What did I do *wrong*?
—You?
—Well it must be me, mustn't it? Or you wouldn't be going off.
—But I've told you, I'm *not* going off as you put it. It's just an extended trip. Don't you see? It can't be more than that, said Bernard simply: Once Miriam gets even a little better I'll just seem boring again.
—But supposing she finds you lovely, said Harriet bursting into tears: I do. Why shouldn't she?
—Oh please! Oh, you promised! You've been so brave. Right through all those coroners' courts, and that vile man bullying us all like criminals. Don't! don't, don't cry now!
Harriet sniffed: It would make you feel wretched, wouldn't it? Well I am rather wretched myself at the moment. Never mind. What do you suppose would happen to Garner?
—Nothing will happen to him at all. He's a bit bored, though. Feels he's been dealt a rotten hand, really. Things aren't *fair,* he says.

Harriet looked in the mirror, straightened her hair and smiled. She had a very solid face, and the smile went right up to her eyes. Bernard smiled too.
—People don't change much, do they? she said.
—No. Give yourself a chance, said Bernard huskily. Listen – the kids are such babies. They'll never notice I'm not there. Don't start being mature and explaining more than you have to. It'll be all right.
—Really? Well, perhaps you'll miss *us,* said Harriet without conviction: Or the flat or the garden or something.
—Of *course* I will. You needn't sort of wait around, said Bernard awkwardly: If you don't want to. Still. I'd be grateful if you gave everything about six months before writing me off.

By the hospital bed-side he felt totally at ease.

—Fermented peach juice? said Miriam, laughing.

—Why not? Just think what old ladies can do with dandelions.

—But they don't *mainline* it, do they? Or have I got England completely wrong? I suppose I may have, said Miriam abstractedly: Bernard, what's that road I'm staring at? Over there, going up the hill?

—The road over the Gogs.

—Yes. What a quiet peaceful rise in the landscape it is, isn't it? I'd forgotten Cambridgeshire *had* any hills.

They were looking out from a window in Addenbrooke's new hospital in mid-afternoon. There were very few cars visible over the hedgerows; and those that could be seen just caught the last rays of winter sunshine like insects.

—They let me have newspapers today. I was quite excited. But it was a great disappointment. They were so familiar right away. I mean nothing seemed to have changed. It was just as though I'd never *been* anywhere.

—Well, said Bernard.

—You aren't supposed to talk about *that*, are you? I know. The only one who's allowed to is a nice young man with rimless glasses who comes round every morning and asks about my dreams, he writes everything down and looks very thoughtful. But it's no use pretending, is it? said Miriam: Something's happened that's not quite ordinary, and today I found out it hasn't just happened inside my head. Listen, bend closer.

Bernard did so.

—A reporter fiddled his way in here this morning. He pretended to be my brother, and the Ward Sisters were just changing shifts. I knew he was a reporter as soon as I set eyes on him, but I let him get away with it.

—Oh dear, said Bernard: That's unfortunate.

—Well no, it was a bit like one of those children's games, where you try and learn what's going on from the

questions that are asked. You know, if someone asks about Miss Prism in the library, then at least *that* rules out –
—Yes, said Bernard agitatedly : I know the game, but what did *he* get from *you*? In the process.
—Not much. On the other hand, I didn't do very well either. Best discovery was what paper he worked for, really, said Miriam : Now. Either I've got a most unusual disease, or else something in the real world is a good deal screwier than I thought.

Their conversation was interrupted by a nurse who came to give Miriam some tea.
—Not too long now, said the nurse, warningly : Not today.
Miriam sighed : No. I've been restless, haven't I? It's all beginning to bug me; this routine, and these people looking after me all the time. Do I get *expelled* if I swear at the night sister? she demanded.
The nurse said : Of course not. But your bloood pressure's *up* again, and we're trying to keep you quiet. That's all.
—Bernard, is it true I'm rich?
—Quite rich. Not in the gossip-columnist range though, I wouldn't have thought.
—And all because of my mother's bits and pieces?
—Yes. They're in the bank. Even the bank insured them.

She stared out into the dropping winter darkness over the Gogs.
—I still don't like this time of day. I don't like the way the light starts to go fuzzy, and then you can't see the trees properly, and suddenly everything goes solid. And disappears. And I'm left looking into darkness. It's like black water. But I don't know why it frightens me so much.
—Think of France. We're going to France.
—Are we though? Are we *really*? I don't know any more. Is he telling the truth? she asked the nurse : Am I really getting out of here in a week or so? It seems so impossible to believe I'd ever get out.

—Just as soon as we get you stabilized; back to normal rhythms, said the nurse briskly.

—I wish I knew what *was* normal for me. All this? What I can remember? Nurse, I think my Circadian clock was always rather to pot, do I have to wait until you've got *that* right?

—I'm going to get a sedative, said the nurse.

—Listen, whispered Bernard quickly when she had gone: I promise I'll tell you the *whole* story next time I come. O.K.? Do you trust me?

—Yes. I don't know why. But you do seem definitely to *exist* out there.

—It's because I'm fat, I expect, said Bernard: Will you take the sedative? When she comes back? Please.

—All right.

He bent over and kissed her.

—I'll speak to the doctor too.

Jenny said, in tones of hushed astonishment: Well, Bernard Hill. Good heavens. It's true then.

—What?

—Well. You know. The rumours had it you were still about.

—Hardly headline stuff, Jenny. It's all open, just ask Harriet. Have you been to see Miriam yet?

—No. I wasn't sure I could bear it.

—Well you can. And it might help her actually. She's still a bit dislocated. Understandably. So I'm trying to establish some kind of bridge over what happened. Do you mind giving me a drink? I know, what she *needs* desperately, to feel safe at all. It's *continuity*: Some sort of inner thread has gone. I suppose the most extraordinary thing, said Bernard: is how easily we all manage to wake with that thread secure every morning. We just pick ourselves up from darkness and carry on. It's remarkable

really. And she has to learn it again to become human.
Will you help? Garner's hopeless, you must see that.
—Well, of course.
—And he gabbles.

Carrying on from darkness, thought Miriam, trying not
to look into the black window, wishing the nurse
would come and roll down the blind. It will always be
there, the darkness. Bernard can't make that go away.
Because it's inside me now. But he is kind, I wonder what
Harriet makes of her life? I ought not to steal him. He's
a good man. I don't deserve that.

I don't *want* to fall asleep. I *never* want to fall asleep
now. I don't know that I ever want to *think* too long, in
case I fall back inside my head again into darkness; and
drift off like a lost kite with nothing to tether me. I must
have a fixed point to hold on to. We all need that, but I
never understood it before. Now I can't bear to know
how we all have to float off wherever it is, into that
silence and darkness, which isn't sleep, and isn't dream
and simply takes every thought we have and swallows us
up. Which is horrible to imagine. If only I could just
live permanently with open eyes, and the ordinary world
about me. Against all sedatives. As long as possible. Like
daylight. If only it were possible.

Jenny and Bernard sat on either side of her bed.
—I see, said Miriam slowly : Except I wonder. What will
happen to Cressida?
—Harriet is launching an appeal, said Jenny : Wouldn't
you know?
—Cressida probably saved your life, said Bernard : There
wouldn't have been any question of criminal proceedings,
after the inquest, if she hadn't been such an execrable

witness. Miriam giggled. Bernard and Jenny exchanged anxious glances.

—I'm sorry, she said penitently : I'm not being callous. I was just imagining how she would be. Have you got a transcript ?

—I could get one, said Bernard uncertainly.

—It's hard to imagine Stavros dead. I thought there must be something like that though. Thank you.

She settled back into the pillows.

—I can rest now.

—Are you still afraid? Of the windows at night? And sleeping ?

—This afternoon was better, said Miriam drowsily.

Something in her voice made both Bernard and Jenny exchange alarm, and Jenny got up quietly to call a nurse.

—Bernard, don't be sad, said Miriam : Last night I dreamt of my mother. It's the first time she's come in her own person. I was very young again and she was giving me medicine. Don't worry, she said, take this. Rest. It'll pass, and I'm here waiting for you. I'll take care of you. There's no need to struggle, or be obstinate. Just lie back, she said and put a cold hand on my forehead. She must have wanted to do that so often. But she never nursed me when I was sick. They wouldn't let her. So it wasn't a memory was it ?

Bernard said : Slow down.

—She said, you need my hand. And I gave her my hand. I think she had a very pure spirit, don't you ?

—Yes, said Bernard : Miriam, listen. The nurse is here.

—Is she ?

—She wants to take your pulse.

Miriam held out her hand : She loved me very much. And I never knew that. But now I know about it, properly, I'm happy. It was such a happy dream, to be a child again.

The nurse said : Lie down, dear. Would one of you call the Sister ? Please.

—Is her temperature up?

—She's fibrillating.

Bernard looked at Miriam's smiling face. She didn't look very ill, certainly. But he could see Jenny frowning over the figures.

—They'll do a cardiograph, she said.

—Will you leave, please? asked the nurse.

—Oh, said Miriam: *Why* can't you let him stay. He's good for me.

—Can I? asked Bernard.

The nurse hesitated. Then she quickly drew the curtain round the three of them. The small machine on rollers came up to the bed tamely. There was nothing frightening about it. Nor about the four sticky pads the nurse attached to Miriam's lovely bare breasts. Miriam held Bernard's hand and smiled at him.

—What's that? said Bernard.

—It's a print-out.

Bernard puzzled over it.

—What are the uneven leaps?

—Well. They shouldn't be there. She'll have to go back on the screen for a day or two. It's a pity. She was so calm this morning.

—I'm calm *now,* said Miriam: Look, it's late afternoon, and I can look right out of the window, and the dark clouds don't frighten me. Yesterday I saw a full moon, and it stared like a single white eye, accusingly. And today I saw how beautiful it was. To have such a cold white globe circling the earth. Even the rain on the hill, when I can see the wind blowing, or the rain up against the window looks so lovely this afternoon. I'm not unhappy. Why do you want to move me?

Bernard showed the print-out to Jenny who said: There is something wrong. It's not anxiety or weakness. It's new. I'm sorry.

—What is?

—Will you come this way, Dr Hill?

—Bernard! cried Miriam: Where are they taking me?

Bernard and Jenny sat grimly on two upright green chairs outside Coronary Care.

—She didn't seem to *mind* about Stavros, said Bernard: *Did* she?

—You asked me that before, reminded Jenny.

—I'm sorry. What did you reply?

—I agreed with you. She didn't seem to mind hearing he was dead.

—I skated over the rest of it. Didn't I?

—Yes. You were very tactful. Don't look so stricken with guilt.

—But it's terrible, said Bernard: I don't think I can bear it if she dies now.

But I'm not frightened. I don't need to run off into an enchanted garden any more. This country will do. Any rotten wet country will do. I don't want to slide away, slide off, hide. I want to be here. Here.

—I'm sorry, said the nurse: It sometimes happens. Just a minor relapse.

—I must see her, said Bernard: Do you realize it's my fault?

—What does he mean? asked the nurse.

—Can't he go in?

—Not now, I'm sorry.

Bernard looked at elegant new furnishings, and scrutinized the imitation oil painting closely for the hundredth time. The chairs looked strange. Particularly the new

158

cream cloth chairs. People sat in those chairs then, while others disappeared. The chairs would outlast many a wait like this. Many people would keep just falling off the planet, and these chairs would go on, fixed and silent. It was unbearable. He hated them. Smug, expensive, permanent. THINGS.

—What are you doing? said the nurse, strangely.

—I'm kicking the chair, said Bernard : How is she?

—You can come now.

—Bernard. Listen. They say I'm going to be fine. Is it true?

Bernard looked up mutely. The nurse nodded her head.

—Yes, he said.

—Do you promise?

—Yes.

—I don't want to sail away.

—Never, he said violently : I won't let you.

Her hand was hot in his, and her eyes were only half-open; the lower half, which gave her a dazed, drunken expression. He looked up enquiringly at the nurse.

—She's asleep now.

—I'm not going.

—She's safe here. You must go. Look at the other patients. Bernard did so, with mute horror. Miriam was so young and so beautiful, and the people lying about her were all forty years older, and grey. Even their flesh was grey.

—Dr Hill, the nurse insisted.

Reluctantly, he released Miriam's hand.

—You don't think she could possibly die? said Bernard : Do you?

They were sitting drinking Nescafé from plastic cups from a machine in the entrance hall.

—Bernard, said Jenny: Even if she doesn't. Die. I think she's going to be pretty sick. Can you face that?

Bernard looked at her in astonishment.

—It just seems a bit one-sided to me, muttered Jenny, awkwardly. Bernard said nothing though the words annoyed him. He could forgive them, he thought. Well, he could forgive anything really. Couldn't he? He didn't need to convince anyone else. After a pause he said: What do you suppose really happened to Stavros' mind?

—They say his best work was scooped by an American when he was still young and trusting. The one who just got a Nobel prize. Now what's his name? Anyway, the story goes Stavros tried his work out on the best English blokes in the field and they more or less laughed him down. So when he met some interest abroad he got a bit reckless. Wrote it all out, probably. It wouldn't be the first time. Some people can stand that kind of thing better than others.

—If they have hobbies? said Bernard, smiling faintly.

—Some kind of life outside their ambitions anyway.

—I see. So perhaps what he was doing to Miriam was a kind of game, finally?

—You know what I meant!

—Of course, exclaimed Bernard: But I understand more now. Stavros was always restless. Most people aren't. I wasn't. That's why I had a very *comfortable* life. So comfortable I can't *remember* it very well. It's not enough, Jenny. I feel absolutely shameless about one thing: there's just got to be more than *that*. Work or not. And Miriam *is* more. For me. I'd settle for a bit of one-sided giving gratefully. Poor Stavros just had too desperate a level of demand.

—Well, Miriam's tough, said Jenny, uncertain of what to say: She's a survivor. I wouldn't put it past her to recover completely.

Bernard dug his nails into his own palms. And waited.